GYM CANDY

by

Carl Deuker

HOUGHTON MIFFLIN HARCOURT
BOSTON   NEW YORK

The author
wishes to thank
Ann Rider, the editor of this
book, for her help and
encouragement.

■ ■ ▪

The text of this book is set in LinoLetter Roman.

Library of Congress Cataloging-in-Publication Data
Deuker, Carl.

Gym candy / by Carl Deuker.

p. cm.

Summary: Groomed by his father to be a star player, football is the only thing that
has ever really mattered to Mick Johnson, who works hard for a spot on the varsity
team his freshman year, then tries to hold on to his edge by using steroids, despite
the consequences to his health and social life.

ISBN-13: 978-0-618-77713-6 (hardcover)

ISBN-13: 978-0-547-07631-7 (paperback)

[1. Football— Fiction. 2. Fathers and sons— Fiction. 3. High schools— Fiction. 4.
Schools— Fiction. 5. Steroids— Fiction. 6. Family life— Washington (State)— Fiction.
7. Washington (State)— Fiction.] I. Title.

PZ7.D493Gym 2007

[Fic]— dc22

2007012749

Manufactured in the United States of America

DOM 10 9 8
4500260563

For Anne and Marian

PART ONE

1

MY EARLIEST MEMORY is of an afternoon in June. I was four years old, and I was in the backyard with my dad. He'd just bought me a purple and gold mini football, my first football. He'd marked off an area of our backyard with a white chalk line. "Here's how it works, Mick. You try to run there," he said, pointing behind the line, "and I try to stop you." He shoved the mini football into the crook of my arm, led me to the far end of the yard, went back to the middle, got down on his knees, and yelled: "Go!"

I took off running toward the end zone. Our backyard is narrow, his arms are long, and even on his knees he could move fast enough to catch a four-year-old. Time after time I ran, trying to get by him. But he never let me have anything for nothing, not even then. Over and over he'd stretch out one of his arms and tackle me. Sometimes the tears would well up. "There's no crying in football," he'd say, which I guess is a joke from some Tom Hanks movie, and he'd send me back to try again.

And then I did it. I zigged when he was expecting a zag, and I was by him. I crossed the chalk line at the end of the yard, my heart pounding. I remember squealing for joy as I turned around. He was lying on the ground, arms reaching toward me, a huge smile on his face. "Touchdown Mick Johnson!" he yelled. "Your first touchdown!"

All those years, I believed that every kid in the neighborhood was jealous of me. And why not? I'd spent time at the houses of the boys on my block—Philip and Cory and Marcus. I'd seen their dads sprawled out on the sofa. Mostly they'd ignore me, but if they asked me something, it was always about school. I'd answer, and then they'd go back to their newspaper. These fathers drove delivery trucks or taught high school or worked in office buildings in downtown Seattle. They wore glasses, had close-cropped hair, and either had bellies or were starting to get them. Everything about them seemed puny.

My dad was bigger and stronger than any of them. His voice was deeper, his smile wider, his laugh louder. Like me, he has red hair, only his was long and reached his shoulders. He wore muscle T-shirts that showed his tattoos—on one shoulder a dragon, on the other a snake. He kept a keg of beer in the den, and whenever he filled his beer stein, he'd let me sip the foam off the top. The way he looked, the way he acted—those things alone put him a million miles above every other kid's father. But there was one last thing that absolutely sealed the deal—my dad was a star.

Our den proved it. It was down in the basement, across from my mom's laundry room, and it was filled with scrapbooks and plaques and medals. Two walls were covered with framed newspaper articles. It was the headlines of those articles that told his story. I used to go downstairs into the den, pick up one of the game balls that he kept in a metal bin in the corner, and walk around and read them, feeling the laces and the leather of the football as I read. MIKE JOHNSON SETS HIGH SCHOOL YARDAGE RECORD . . . MIKE JOHNSON LEADS HUSKIES OVER USC . . . MIKE JOHNSON NAMED TO ALL–PAC TEN FIRST TEAM . . . MIKE JOHNSON SELECTED IN THIRD ROUND.

Sometimes my dad would come in while I was staring at the walls. He'd tell me about a touchdown run he'd made in a rainstorm against Cal or the swing pass in the Sun Bowl that he'd broken for sixty-five yards. When he finished with one of his stories, he'd point to the two bare walls. "Those are yours, Mick," he'd say. "You're going to fill them up with your own headlines."

My mom had been a top gymnast at the University of Washington the same years my dad was on the football team. She runs around Green Lake every morning, and she used to do the Seattle-to-Portland bicycle race, so she knows all about competition. But every time she heard my dad talk about me making the headlines, she'd put her hands on my shoulders and look at me with her dark eyes. "You don't have to fill any walls with anything," she'd say. "You just be you." Then she'd point her finger at my dad. "And you stop with all that 'bare walls' stuff."

My dad would laugh. "A little pressure is good for a boy. Keeps him on his toes."

2

I STARTED KINDERGARTEN a year later than most kids, so all my life I've been older than my classmates. When kids hear you're a year older, they assume you're stupid, but my mom says I knew my numbers and most of the letters of the alphabet and that I was ready for school. Holding me out was my dad's idea.

I don't really remember too much about it, other than that I was sad because I had to spend the mornings at Ballard Lutheran Preschool and wouldn't get a metal lunch pail like Cory Ginski, who was going to North Beach Elementary. I started crying about that at dinner, and my dad took me aside and told me I'd have an edge later on.

I didn't understand what he was talking about then, but I figured it out once I started Pop Warner football in third grade. My dad petitioned the league to let me play on a team with my classmates even though I was older, and his petition was approved. The rest of the kids in my class were trying to figure out which way they were going, but my dad had taught me how to cut back against the grain, how to reverse fields, how to straight-arm tacklers. Add to that the extra year I had on everyone and it was no contest: I was a star in Pop Warner from day one.

I loved it. Who wouldn't? I scored a bunch of touchdowns, made the all-league teams, got the MVP trophies at the team banquets. Ninety-nine percent of the time I didn't think about being older than the kids I was playing against. But every once in a while I'd remember, and my body would tense up and my face would redden. I thought about asking my dad to let me play in my real age bracket, but I never did.

In the off-season, my dad would sign me up for every football camp he could find, even if it meant driving hours to get there. As I got older, he set up more and more football equipment in our yard. Blocking sleds, nets, tires for agility drills. My mom didn't like it that everything was football, football, football. "Mick needs some balance in his life," she'd say.

"What would you like him to do?" my dad would answer. "He's going to be way too big for gymnastics."

"I don't know. But something other than football three hundred and sixty-five days a year."

Whenever they had that argument, my dad always turned to me. "Do you want to turn out for soccer this year, Mick?" he'd ask.

I'd shake my head.

"How about basketball or baseball?"

"No," I'd say.

"Chess? The Math Olympiad?"

"I just want to play football."

My dad would smile; my mom would shake her head; and that would be the end of it—for a while.

It was true what I said—that I loved football. But something else was true, too. I'd played basketball a little, played baseball a little, played soccer a little. I'd played them all enough to know that I was nothing special in any of them and never would be. If I was going to make my mark, it was going to be on the football field.

3

YOU CAN GO ALONG THINKING your dad's perfect for a long time, but not forever. I don't know exactly when I started to figure out that everything didn't add up. Maybe fourth or fifth grade, but for sure by middle school I knew.

My mom worked at a bank in the loan department. She worked regular hours like everybody else's parents. But my dad's job was different, which was why he was the one who took me to practices and why he was home most days after school.

He had the early shift—five to ten in the morning—at a talk radio station that covered sports twenty-four hours a day. The show was called *Ben in the A.M.* Ben Braun was the host and did seventy-five percent of the talking. My dad was the second guy. "I fill in when Ben runs out of things to say," he said, explaining his job to Grandpa Leo one Christmas. "But, let me tell you, that isn't too often."

Ben Braun had been to our house a few times, but only a few, because my mom didn't like him. He was a little guy with strangely short arms, a loud voice, and a louder laugh. He talked with his mouth full of food, and when he told a joke, he'd bang his fist down on the table, making the silverware jump. "The man is obnoxious," my mom said every time after he left. "Absolutely obnoxious."

"He's my boss," my dad would say. "We've got to invite him over sometimes."

Ben Braun had never played any sport, so I didn't understand why he talked so much while my dad said so little. "He's got the radio voice and he's got the college degree," my dad explained when I asked him about it. "That's the way it works."

I tried to listen to the show before I went to school. I wanted to like it, but I had trouble following it. Sometimes they'd talk about movie stars or singers for ten minutes straight. One thing I did notice. Instead of calling my dad "Mike," lots of times Ben Braun would say: "Let's see what Mr. Third-Rounder has to say about that," and then he'd laugh that big laugh of his.

I'd probably heard him call my dad "Mr. Third-Rounder" a dozen times before I asked my mom why he did that. She flushed red. "Because Ben Braun is a mean man," she said. "A mean man with a cruel sense of humor. I wish your father didn't have to work with him, and I wish you wouldn't listen to him."

I didn't say anything more. I knew she didn't want to talk about it, whatever it was. But all day at school, I thought about it. *Mr. Third-Rounder . . . Mr. Third-Rounder . . . Mr. Third-Rounder.*

After school that day, I went downstairs to the den and looked once more at the framed headlines. The last one read MIKE JOHNSON SELECTED IN THIRD ROUND. That had always been my favorite headline because it meant that my dad had made it to the NFL. So what was funny about it? What was Ben Braun laughing at?

I stared at the headline and stared at it, and then, I got it—I got Ben Braun's joke. The wall next to that framed article was bare—it was my wall to fill. But that's what was wrong—that bare wall. It had always been wrong, and for a long time some part of me had known it. I followed the NFL. First-round picks are absolute locks to make it. But to be selected in the third round, you still have to be one of the best college football players in the nation. Joe Montana, the greatest quarterback of all time, was a third-round draft choice. My dad should have played professional football for ten years. The bare wall should have been full of NFL headlines, but there wasn't one. He'd grabbed the headlines in college; as a pro he'd done nothing.

I climbed back upstairs. My dad was in the kitchen, sitting on a stool, eating peanuts. "I thought I heard you come in," he said. "How about we go to the park,

11

throw the ball around a little? I want to give you practice catching balls that come to you over the wrong shoulder."

"Yeah, sure," I said, but instead of moving, I just stood.

"Well," he said, reaching for his jacket, "are we going?"

"Dad, did you ever play for the Chargers?"

He put the jacket down. "I got drafted by the Chargers. Third round. You know that."

"But did you ever play?"

"A couple of preseason games. Yeah."

"And then what happened?"

His voice went flat. "Then I sprained my ankle. A high ankle sprain, the worst kind. My foot turned purple from my toe to my calf. I tried to come back too early, and I resprained it. The Chargers kept me on their injured reserve list, hoping I'd recover, but it never came around. It still isn't right."

"So it was an injury. That's why you didn't play."

"I just told you. Why all the questions?"

"No reason."

We went to the park then, but he didn't pay much attention to what I was doing, didn't offer suggestions. We quit after half an hour.

After dinner, I half watched television, half played

video games, and then took a shower and went to bed. Around nine-thirty, my mom came in to say good night, which was normal. Later, I was almost asleep when the door opened again and my father came in, which wasn't.

"You awake, Mick?" he said as he sat down on the edge of the bed.

"Yeah, Dad," I said. "I'm awake."

For a while he just sat. When he finally spoke, his voice was low. "I don't want you to think my NFL career amounted to nothing, because that's not true. The house you're living in? The bed you're sleeping on? The furniture? You know who bought those things?" He tapped himself on the chest. "I bought them, that's who. And do you know how I bought them? I bought everything with my money from the San Diego Chargers. Five hundred thousand dollars, that's what my signing bonus was. That's NFL money. Money I made as a professional football player. A half million dollars. That's not nothing, Mick, and don't ever let anybody tell you it is. You understand what I'm saying?"

"Yeah, I understand," I said, a little frightened of him.

"All right then," he said. "Go to sleep."

After he left I lay in the dark, confused not by what he had said but by what he hadn't. For the first time I understood that deep down inside my dad was un-happy.

I'd always bragged some to the guys at school and on my teams about what a great football player my dad had been. It makes no sense, but after that night I bragged more than ever. Every one of his stories grew in my retelling. If he told me he broke four tackles and scampered thirty-three yards against Stanford, or turned a five-yard swing pass into a twenty-five-yard touchdown against Oregon, then I told my friends that he broke six tackles and raced forty-eight yards against Stanford and broke a sixty-yard touchdown pass against Oregon. You'd think I would have kept my mouth shut.

4

IN SEVENTH GRADE my teacher, Mr. Pengilly—a little guy with a wispy beard that made him look like a goat—had us write about our favorite activity. Mine was football, of course. I wrote that it was fun and that I liked to score touchdowns and hear people cheer for me. I turned it in, and a week later I got it back with an F at the top. "You need to make the game come alive," he had written in the margin. "This is dead."

I've never been a great student, but I'm a good student, and that was the first F I'd ever gotten on anything. I was mad, and all through class I glared at him. What did he know about football? Nothing. When the bell rang I headed to the door, but Mr. Pengilly's voice stopped me. "Come here, Mick," he said.

I marched over to his desk.

"You didn't like that grade?"

"No, I didn't."

"You can redo the paper, you know."

"Football is what I like," I said.

"You don't have to change your topic. Just make me feel what you feel when you're playing. What you've written could apply to Ping-Pong or ice dancing. Tell me what's different about football."

"I don't know what's different about it," I muttered.

"Sure you do, Mick. You just need to think more before you write."

On my way out, I threw my paper into the trash and tried to forget about it. But I couldn't. So that night I did what Pengilly told me to do—I thought it through. And I realized that what I'd written was junk. Worse than junk, because most of it was a lie. Football isn't fun; it's hard work. The drills are grueling and the games are worse. The risk of injury is there on every play, and even if you don't get hurt, when you wake up the morning after a game your whole body feels as if it's been put through a huge washing machine. And running backs—my position—have it worst of all. For a running back, every game is like being in a street fight with the numbers stacked against you. You're trying to take the ball up the field, and all the guys on defense have the same goal—and it's not just to stop you. They want to punish you; they want to make you pay in blood for every inch you gain.

And there it was—the reason I love the game. I love it because it is so hard. I love it because every single play is a challenge of every single part of me—body and mind. Being physically tough isn't enough. Lots of tough guys quit football. You have to be mentally tough to keep going when every muscle in your body is screaming: "Stop!"

But if you don't stop, if you make yourself stay out there, if you take on the challenge—the payoff is unreal. I thought back to my best runs, my greatest moments. On some of them, it was as if I were a hummingbird, darting through tiny holes, breaking into the open, flying down the field for a touchdown. On others, I felt more like a bull, crashing straight ahead, legs churning, fighting for inches. And on the best, I was the bullet coming out of the barrel of a gun. That's the thrill of football, that's what makes it better than any other game—the speed and the power, the shifting from one to the other, the fighting through the pain, the fighting through the fear, the coming out on the other side, ball above my head, crowd roaring: *Touchdown! Touchdown! Touchdown!*

I took out a piece of paper and wrote it all down as fast as I could, afraid I'd forget it. The next day I turned my paper in to Mr. Pengilly, and the day after that he gave it back with an A+ on the top. "I felt it this time," he had written.

5

SOMETIMES I THINK I should have given that paper to my mom, because that was the year she stopped coming to my games. I knew she never really liked them; I knew she was afraid I'd get hurt; I knew she'd felt the same way when my dad had played. Still, she'd always been there.

That changed after the last game of my seventh grade season in Pop Warner. My team was behind 20–16 with less than a minute left. Our defense had stopped the Magnolia team around the fifty-yard line, and my coach sent me in to return the punt. "We need a big runback," he screamed.

The punt was high and short—dangerous to return because a slew of tacklers would be in my face. Any other time I would have played it safe and let the ball bounce, but the coach was right about needing a good runback, and I wanted to win. So I raced up and caught the ball on the dead run. I'd taken one step when one of the guys on the other team leveled me, driving his shoulder right into my gut. My helmet popped off my head and I went down as if I'd been shot. They had to use smelling salts to get me to my feet.

At home I took a long, long shower. My gut was so sore that I had to lean forward to walk. There was absolutely no way I could eat any dinner. So I hobbled into my room, stretched out on my bed, and turned the TV to ESPN. I didn't even know what game was on, because I was in too much pain to pay attention. Instead, I let my eyes wander over all the posters of running backs I have in my room. They go from wall to wall and even cover the ceiling: Jim Brown, Gale Sayers, Eric Dickerson, Emmitt Smith, Barry Sanders—you name him and I've got a poster. I closed my eyes and pictured each of them in action—the pure power of Brown, the grace of Payton, the high knees of Sayers—and then pictured myself doing the same things, pictured a poster of me up there on the wall next to them. My little daydream ended when I heard a tap on the door. A second later, my mother pushed it open. "Can I come in?" she said.

"Sure," I said.

She sat at the foot of the bed. "How do you feel?"

"I'm okay," I said. "Just sore."

She reached over and ran her hand across my forehead, pushing my hair back. I pulled away from her touch, embarrassed to be treated like a child. She took her hand away and then followed my eyes to the posters. "You're not going to quit, are you?"

"Quit what?"

"Football."

"Why would I quit football?" I asked. Then I understood. "Just because of that tackle? Mom, that was no big deal. I'm okay. I got my bell rung. It's part of the game."

She nodded. "I knew you'd say that. It's exactly what your father would say." She paused. "Mick, I love you and I want to be part of your life, but I can't go to your football games anymore. I just can't. Every time you get tackled, I'm afraid you're going to be paralyzed, or even killed. I want to run out on the field and grab you and pull you off."

"That's crazy," I said. "Nothing like that is going to happen."

"Mick, things like that do happen."

"Well, they aren't going to happen to me." I looked at her and saw that her eyes were filling with tears. "It's okay, Mom," I said quickly. "You don't have to come to my games. I'll tell you about them afterward. Or if you don't want to even hear about them, that's okay, too. Really."

She leaned forward and kissed me on the head. "You can tell me about them," she said. "I just wanted you to know why I won't be there anymore."

After my mom left, I tried to imagine quitting football the way she wanted, but I couldn't. What would I do if I didn't play football? I had nothing else that I cared about. Even more, who would I be if I didn't play football? The game was in my DNA; I needed it as much as I needed air to breathe.

6

MR. KNECHT HAD BEEN my Pop Warner coach for years, but in eighth grade his son, Joey Knecht, quit playing. Our new coach was Mr. Rooney, a guy about my dad's age who'd played college ball at Oregon State. I liked Mr. Knecht okay, but I was excited when I heard we were getting a new coach.

The first day Rooney had us line up on the fifty-yard line. He'd call a name, and that guy would step forward, and he asked a few questions—the typical stuff. Finally it was my turn. "Mick Johnson," he said.

I stepped forward and gave a little wave. "Here," I said.

He looked down at his clipboard and then looked back at me. "You're the old kid, right? The one who should be in high school? The one playing on an exemption?"

It was like being hit in the face. I was totally embarrassed, totally humiliated. Most of the guys on the team didn't know I was older, and the few who did had known for so long it was almost as if they didn't know. Rooney brought it back, and the way he said it made it seem as though I was a cheater.

"I started kindergarten a year late," I said. "My dad thought—"

"Are you Mike Johnson's kid? The guy who played for the Huskies." He said it as if it was something to be ashamed of.

I nodded.

"All right, Johnson. You don't have to give me your life story, though I'm sure it's fascinating. What position do you play?"

"Running back."

He snorted. "Figures."

. . .

Practice was like every other first practice. We did a lot of simple drills, ran a bunch, and stretched a bunch. Only for me it was different. Mr. Knecht had always praised everything I did. I'd always be the one who demonstrated how something was supposed to be done. For Rooney nothing I did was good enough. He wouldn't even call me by my name. I was "Red" to him. "Pick it up, Red," he'd say, or "Pay attention, Red." I hated being called Red, and the more he did it the more I hated him.

After practice my dad asked about the new coach. When I complained about him, my dad closed his eyes and scratched the top of his head. "Rooney . . . Rooney . . . Rooney. I think I remember him. It seems to me there was some play where I ran over him and into the end zone. It ended up on *SportsCenter*." My dad laughed. "That's why the guy doesn't like you. He's still feeling the pain. Just ignore him."

But I couldn't ignore him, because he kept calling me Red, and every time he did, I could taste the anger. Always, in every camp and on every team, I'd been the hard worker, the guy who did everything by the book. But I wasn't that way with Rooney. He was disrespecting me, so that's what he got back. If he told us to get in a perfectly straight line for some drill, I made sure I had one foot sticking out six inches. If he told us to listen up, I always turned my shoulders to the side and looked off across the field; if he told us our break was over, I always took one more slug from my water bottle. Rooney would see, and glower, but what could he do? I was his best running back. You can't bench your best running back for a little twitch of the mouth.

There were two new kids on the team. One of them, Gerard Sampson, quit after the first day. The other was Drew Carney, a funny-looking kid with big ears. Drew played quarterback, had great size and strength, and had a gun for an arm. The guy was a player, and from day one Rooney loved him.

Whenever Rooney blew his whistle, Drew was always the first one in line. In every drill, Drew gave one hundred and ten percent. All through those early practice sessions Rooney would single Drew out and tell the rest of us that we should try to be like him.

One Friday, after I'd loafed during a blocking drill, Rooney pointed a stubby finger at me: "You there, Red. I want you to pull the towel against Drew. The rest of you guys—form a circle and watch. I want you to see this."

Pulling the towel was Rooney's favorite drill. It was basically tug of war, only it was one-on-one instead of in teams. But the *watching* part was different. Always before, we'd each had our own partner and we'd been all tugging and sweating simultaneously. Only you and your partner would know who won.

Rooney had us face off at the fifty-yard line. The object was simple: pull the other guy completely over the line. I took hold of one end of the towel; Drew grabbed the other. I looked toward Rooney, but before I was ready, he blew his whistle. A split second later I was lying face-down in the dirt on Drew's side of the fifty. The guys circled around laughed. Rooney glared down.

"That wasn't fair," I said. "I wasn't ready."

"You're never ready," Rooney barked. "Go ahead. Pick up the towel. Try again."

I took my end of the towel and grabbed it as tightly as I could. I didn't look to Rooney this time; I kept my eyes on Drew. The whistle blew. I dug my heels into the ground and pulled. My arms started aching; my legs started cramping. I tried to turn just a bit, but in that split second something happened, because for the second time I was lying face first in front of Drew, and for the second time everyone was laughing.

"You want to go a third time?" Rooney said.

I shook my head.

"I didn't think you would. You're Mike Johnson's son through and through. You're going to end up just like your father. The talent of an all-star, the attitude of a punk. I've seen that smirk on your face for too long. I've seen it and I'm sick of it. I'm not having bad actors poisoning my team. So you think it over, Mr. All-Star Mick Johnson. You want to play for me, then you practice the way I want you to practice. If not, don't come back. Now go sit in the bleachers until the end of practice."

I went to the bleachers and sat, my hands clenched in fists, a lump in my throat. I wanted to hit Rooney for what he'd said and for what he'd done. It wasn't my fault he was a lousy linebacker; it wasn't my fault my dad had humiliated him on the field. Why was he taking it out on me?

Finally the whistle blew, ending practice. As I headed to the parking lot, my dad pulled in. I threw my duffel into the back of his Jeep Wrangler and climbed in. "Bad day?" he said.

"I'm quitting," I said. "I hate Rooney."

He pulled out of the lot. "What happened?"

"Nothing happened. Rooney doesn't know anything about football, that's all. He's stupid and I'm quitting."

He drove in silence for a while. At a red light, he looked over at me. "You need to play on a team, Mick."

"Then I'll play on another team," I said.

"You can't play on another team. The teams are set by where you live. It's Rooney's team or no team, and you're not quitting. So get over it, whatever it is."

7

AS SOON AS WE WALKED in the door, the phone rang. It was Bull Tinsley, one of my dad's old football friends. Tinsley had extra tickets for the Mariners game. My dad put his hand over the receiver and turned to me. "He's got one for you, too," he said. "You coming?"

I shook my head.

I didn't eat much at dinner. After my dad left for the game, I went upstairs to my room, took out my Game Boy, and sat on my bed holding it, not even turning it on. I kept thinking about what Rooney had said about my dad: *The talent of an all-star, the attitude of a punk.*

What did he mean? What was he talking about?

Around nine I opened my bedroom door, stepped out into the hallway, and tiptoed downstairs. In the living room my mom was drinking tea and watching a Christian television channel. I went back upstairs and turned on the radio. The Mariners game was only in the sixth inning. My dad wouldn't be home for hours.

I slipped into the computer room. I'd done searches on all sorts of things before, but I'd never done one on my dad. I'd never even thought of doing one on him. I had his trophies, his pictures, his scrapbooks.

I opened up Google and typed in "Mike Johnson San Diego Charger running back." I hit Return and the screen filled with sites. I read down, searching for one that fit. And there it was. The dates and names matched.

I clicked on it and was taken to an article from the *San Diego Union Tribune*. The headline read ROOKIE GIVEN UNCONDITIONAL RELEASE. I read through it, slowly. Lots of it I knew. The career as a Washington Husky. The selection in the third round.

But after that, everything was new. All through the Chargers training camp, my dad had been in trouble. There had been fights with teammates and arguments with coaches. There had been missed team meetings, an arrest for drunk driving, and another arrest at a dance club in Tijuana. On the football field in the pre-season games, there were blown blocking assignments, fumbles on kickoffs, personal fouls. "He just didn't have what it takes to succeed in the NFL," the coach said, explaining why he'd cut my dad. "It's as simple as that."

8

I DIDN'T SLEEP MUCH that night. I lay on my bed, confused and angry. That stuff my dad had said about an ankle injury—it was a lie. How many times had I told my teammates what a great running back he'd been as a Husky? How many times had I said that if he hadn't been injured, he'd have been a star in the NFL? How many of them had known the truth? Some of their fathers must have known all along. They must have followed his career as a Husky and his flameout in the NFL. They'd have told their sons. And if some of my teammates knew, that meant all of them knew. Kids probably talked about my dad and me all the time, talked about us and laughed.

I woke up early the next morning, ate breakfast by myself, and then returned to my room, shut my door, and just sat on my bed, being mad all over. Around ten my dad knocked. "You want to toss the ball around?"

"I don't feel like it," I said through the locked door.

"You're not quitting, Mick. I mean it."

"I just don't feel like playing football right now. I'll play later."

He went away, and I thought what a hypocrite he was, telling me that I had to play. What had he done? Drunk, and missed meetings, and gotten in trouble with strippers in Mexico. He was married to my mom then, too. She had told me that they got married while they were still in college.

A few minutes later he was back at my door, only this time he was pounding. "Get out here, Mick," he said. "Right now."

"I'll play catch later," I shouted.

"I'm not talking about that. I want this door open now."

He was mad, but I was mad, too. I stomped across my room and opened the door. "What?" I said.

He grabbed my arm, yanked me into the spare bedroom, and pointed to the computer. "Have you been checking on me?"

My face went red. "No," I said.

"No? Then what's this?"

The browser was open. He moved the mouse until the cursor hovered over Go. He dragged the cursor down to History and then he clicked. A couple of clicks more and the *San Diego Union Tribune* article was on the screen. "So tell me again—you weren't checking on me?"

"I wanted to find out the real reason you never played in the NFL."

There, I had said it.

"So you go snooping behind my back?"

My mom must have heard shouting because she'd come upstairs and was standing behind him. "Leave him alone, Mike. He had to find out."

My father kept his eyes on me. "You think I'm a failure, don't you? You read one article written sixteen years ago and you think I'm a failure?"

"I never said that."

"Yeah? Well, that's what you're thinking, isn't it?"

"Stop badgering him, Mike."

"I'm not badgering him. I'm asking him a question."

"You are badgering him."

He glared at her, and then he walked quickly down the stairs. My mom and I listened as the front door opened, then slammed shut. His Jeep started up and we heard him drive off, fast.

9

ONCE HE WAS GONE, my mom went downstairs and I returned to my room. I picked up my Game Boy, but there was no way I could play anything. Around noon, my mom called me down to lunch. Everything looked the way it always did: The cut flowers were in the vase in the center of the cream-colored table in the kitchen. My sandwich, a sliced apple, and a chocolate chip cookie sat perfectly arranged on a rose-patterned plate. A glass of milk was just to the right. Across from my food were my mom's bowl of plain yogurt with blueberries and her cup of tea. Everything neat and tidy, the way she liked it.

I managed to eat half of the sandwich and most of the apple. She finished about the same amount of her lunch. When I was done, I scraped my plate clean and put it in the sink. I turned to go back upstairs, but my mom stopped me. "Sit down a minute, Mick. There's something you need to hear."

I sat.

For a moment she looked out the window at our rosebush. Then she turned back to me. "All those things you found out on the Internet, I know they hurt you. But your dad didn't kill anybody. He didn't rob a bank or burn down a building. I want you to remember that it's just football. Okay? Just a game."

I started to answer, then stopped.

"What?" she said.

I shook my head. "Nothing."

"Tell me."

"It's more than a game to him, Mom," I said. "And it's more than a game to me, too."

She frowned. "Only if you let it be, Mick."

. .

My dad didn't come home for dinner that night, but my mom told me not to worry. "He called. He drove up into the mountains, to Roslyn. I told him to rent a cabin and stay the night. He'll be back tomorrow."

I ate half a hamburger for dinner. Afterward, I kept going through what I was going to say to him when he came back. I'd try not to be mad at him, and for a while I'd convince myself that my mom was right, but then I'd get mad at him all over again. All that stuff about his ankle sprain. He should have told me the truth.

He returned Sunday afternoon. We ate lunch together, a fresh bunch of flowers in the center of the table. My mom acted as if everything were normal, but he was stiff, like a stranger, and my stomach was in knots. I was afraid I'd throw up if I ate, but I was afraid if I didn't eat he'd ask me what was wrong. I picked at the cheese sandwich, ate most of a banana, and drank half my milk. After lunch I started back up the stairs to my room, but his voice stopped me. "Let's go for a drive, Mick," he said.

His Wrangler is a hardtop, but with the windows down plenty of fresh air blows through. He drove out across the Aurora Bridge, to West Seattle, and down to Alki Beach. On the way we talked about nothing: the sunshine, the Seahawks, the Mariners.

He parked along the water at Alki. We walked on the pathway above the beach for a half-mile or so. Then he spotted a picnic table. "Let's sit down," he said. Puget Sound was a glittering dark blue, its islands a dark green, the sky dotted with puffy white clouds. It was an incredible day, and I couldn't have felt worse.

We sat across from each other. He had a toothpick in his mouth, and he'd chew on it a little, then take it out, and then chew on it some more. Finally he flicked it onto the beach. "That article you read? Everything in it was true. I was a screw-off, and it didn't start with the Chargers. All through high school and college, I dogged practices, was late for meetings—had no work ethic at all. None. But I was the best running back around by far, so when game time came around, the coaches found a way to get me on the field. Then I got to the pros, where there were guys as good as me. I pulled the same crap, and the Chargers got rid of me just like that." He snapped his fingers. "I couldn't believe it. Sometimes I still can't believe it.

"So I came back to Seattle, my tail between my legs. I managed to land a job on sports radio, and a few years later you were born. That was quite a moment, seeing you. I looked in your crib and I thought: *He's not going to end up like me, wasting his talent.*

"I know I've worked you hard all these years. Your mom says I put too much pressure on you, and I guess I do. But you're good at football, Mick. Really, really good. I don't want you to get so mad at me over this that you quit."

I shook my head. "I'm not going to quit. I love football. It's just . . ."

"Just what?" he said.

"It's just that I don't get why you didn't tell me earlier."

He laughed grimly. "That's easy, Mick. Everybody I see at the radio station, friends of your mom's, friends of mine, they look at me and they think: *There's Mike Johnson. He could have been great.* You looked at me and your eyes said: *That's my dad. He is great."* He paused. "I couldn't give it up."

We sat for a little longer, neither of us saying anything. Finally, he stood. "So, we're okay?"

"Yeah," I said. "We're okay."

"We'll still throw the ball around now and again."

"Yeah, we'll still throw the ball around."

On the drive home, neither of us spoke. I don't know what I thought. I didn't hate him; I wasn't really even angry. But things would never be the same. He'd never be as big in my eyes as he'd been, never take up so much of my world.

After that he still gave me advice on technique and strategy, and we still tossed the ball around the park, though we didn't do that as much. The change wasn't in what we did but in what we didn't say. He never again described the big plays he'd made on the football field, and I never again asked him about them. They were all in the past, buried. It was unspoken, but we both understood that the games that mattered were the games yet to be played—my games.

PART TWO

1

So MUCH HAD HAPPENED over that weekend that I forgot how angry Rooney had been until I returned to the practice field Monday. I considered telling him that I was going to stop smarting off, that I was different from my dad, but what good are words? I'd show him.

That practice, I pushed myself to outperform everyone, especially Drew Carney. Running drills, agility drills, strength drills—I took him on. If he made it through the tires in twenty seconds, then I was going to do it in nineteen. If he managed thirty pushups, then I was doing thirty-one. If he ran the four-forty in fifty-five seconds, then I was clocking fifty-four. After two hours, Rooney blew his whistle. "Good practice, men," he called out. He turned to me, and our eyes locked. "Very good practice."

As I walked toward the parking lot, Drew fell in stride beside me. "That was fun," he said.

"What?" I said.

"You trying hard like that—it made practice better."

"Yeah, I guess it did," I said.

"A bunch of us play flag football at Crown Hill Park in the afternoons. A kid named DeShawn Free is always there and usually there are some other guys who go to Shilshole High. You should come around."

. . .

After I ate lunch, I walked to Crown Hill Park. They had even teams, but Drew made the other guys make room for me, even though it meant going six on five. I had a great time that day, and after that I played flag football with those guys every chance I got. The games turned out to be more competitive than our league games. About half the guys were on the Shilshole High varsity, and they were determined to push me and Drew and DeShawn around, which made us determined not to be pushed around. We kicked our effort up a notch, and pretty soon Drew and I started clicking together. Handoffs, pitchouts, swing passes—you name it and we were right in sync. It was as if we'd been playing together all our lives.

That harmony should have carried over and made us tough to beat in Pop Warner, but the league has a rule requiring the coach to play everyone on the team for at least one quarter. Most of our second-stringers were new to football, and it showed.

When Drew was at quarterback and I was at running back, we'd march down the field, slicing through the defense. But at the start of the third quarter, Rooney pulled us, and we'd stand on the sidelines and watch the other team demolish our second string. Sometimes when we came back into the game at the start of the fourth quarter we'd rekindle the fire and win. But lots of the time we'd never find our rhythm. Drew would throw an interception or I'd fumble and our opponents would sneak away with a victory.

After we'd lost some game we should have won, my dad would be stone-faced, his eyes angry. That was okay with Drew and me, because that's exactly how we felt. But Drew's dad would come over, a big smile on his face, and talk about how exciting the game had been. "Sportsmanship, that's what is important, boys. The winning and the losing don't matter."

He was hard to listen to, because it did matter, and not just for our league record. We cared about that, but we were also looking a year ahead. Off and on during the season, a man had shown up at our games. For a quarter, sometimes even a half, he'd stand right next to Mr. Rooney, talking to him and then writing things in a notebook.

Brad Middleton, one of the high school guys we played flag football with, filled us in. "Tall guy, right?

Going bald. That's Mr. Trahane. He's Shilshole High's defensive backfield coach. He's scouting you. You impress him, and you'll get an invitation to spring football, which means you have a solid chance to make the varsity. You don't catch his eye, you won't get invited, and that means the JV team." Middleton paused. "Believe me, you really don't want to be on the JV team. The coach sucks, the practice field sucks, the refs suck, and the team sucks."

Once I knew the score, every game became a tryout. Win or lose, I'd ask my dad if Trahane had been there. If the answer was yes, I'd pepper him with questions. How had I done while he was watching? Did I mess anything up? What did he think Trahane wrote down about me?

"Just keep working hard, like you're doing," my dad would say. "You're not going to get the invite because of one play, and you're not going to lose it because of one play. You try to do too much, and you'll fall flat on your face."

2

W**E FINISHED THE SEASON** with a 5-5 record, just out of
the playoffs. When Pop Warner ended, it was hard to fill
the days. School took up six hours. After school Drew
and I would go to Crown Hill Park to play football, but
each day was shorter and darker than the one before,
and fewer guys were showing up. Weekends were a little better. The field was growing soft from the rain, so
we'd play tackle football in the mud. The grosser it was,
the better. We'd go home, get cleaned up, and then either Drew would come to my house or I'd go to his. We'd
hang out together playing video games and foosball.

Over Christmas break my grandparents came up
from San Francisco and stayed with us for five days.
They're my mom's parents, and they're nice enough,
but they still treat me like I'm five years old. I'd turned
fifteen just before they arrived, and they insisted on
taking me out for a Happy Meal at McDonald's. After
that Grandpa Leo and I went to Interbay to play miniature golf. The wind was howling so hard, I thought it
was going to knock Grandpa Leo into one of the wind-
mills, but he kept telling me how much fun he was
having and how glad he was to be visiting and how
much I had grown. Christmas Day I got the regular

stuff plus my own cell phone. "It's a pay-as-you-go plan, Mick," my mom said. "Strictly for emergencies."

The first week of January, my dad was offered a different time slot at the station. He'd be working with Lion Terry, not Ben Braun, and his hours would be from four in the afternoon to nine at night. My mom wanted him to take it. "You know what I think of Ben Braun," she said.

"Lion would be easier to work with," he said, "and I wouldn't have to get up at four in the morning anymore." He looked at me. "But I won't be around much in the evenings. The house will be empty when you come home."

"That's okay," I said. "I just come in and go right out. You know that."

He pulled on his ear a little. "How about football? How are you going to get to games?"

"I can get a ride with Drew's dad anytime," I said. "He's told me that."

"Take the job," my mom said. "Please."

He smiled. "Ben Braun is not going to be happy."

My mom laughed. "One more reason to take it."

3

Janaury, February, March—all through those months I felt as if I were stuck in mud. Guys had stopped showing up at the park, so the flag football games had fallen apart; the days were short, rainy, and cold; and I was sick of Lowell Middle School, sick of the teachers and the buildings and the kids.

The only person I wasn't sick of was Drew. He and I had had our eyes fixed on spring football since the day Middleton had clued us in about Trahane. I thought about spring football all the time, and I'd bet anything Drew did, too, but through those months we never talked about it. May seemed a long way off, and neither of us wanted to jinx anything. When April came, though, spring football was all we talked about.

I was sure Drew would be invited, and I told him so. He had size and strength, and he was a natural leader. Even in the flag football games, playing with older kids, Drew took command of the huddle. Once I'd gone through all the reasons that he was a lock to get invited, he'd do the same for me. "You've got speed and power, Mick. And you know the game so much better than anyone. You see things other people don't. I wish my dad had taught me half of what you've learned from yours. You've got the football I.Q. of Einstein."

When I was with him, when we were talking, I'd feel good about my chances, but when I was alone, all I could remember were the plays I'd screwed up.

It was the last Monday in April. I was just about to head off to Crown Hill Park when the phone rang. I picked it up, pencil in hand, ready to take a message for my mom or my dad. "This is Mr. Downs, head football coach at Shilshole High," the voice said. "Is Mick Johnson at home?"

My heart was thumping. "This is Mick Johnson."

"Mick, Mr. Trahane watched your Pop Warner football team off and on in the fall. Maybe you were aware of that."

"Yeah," I said. "I mean, sort of." I stopped, confused.

"Well, Mr. Trahane tells me that you are a promising player. Mr. Rooney says your attitude and practice habits are good. We start spring football here at Shilshole High next week. I'd like you to participate. I want to be clear, though. This invitation doesn't mean you are on the varsity. It just means you are working with the varsity. How's that sound?"

"That sounds great," I said, my mouth so dry, I could hardly talk. "That sounds tremendous."

He laughed. "All right, then. You know where the school is?"

"Sure, I know. What time?"

"Three-fifteen. See you there."

"Coach Downs," I said, before he could hang up, "did Mr. Trahane tell you about Drew Carney? He was our quarterback, and—"

"Yes, I know all about Drew. I'll be calling him today, too."

I hung up the phone and sat, staring straight ahead.

I was going to get my chance.

4

THAT GLOW LASTED all the way to Sunday night. But by the time I went to bed, a tiny bit of fear had crept into my head, and that fear grew and grew until by Monday afternoon it had crowded out everything else. My dad had warned me that it was going to happen. "You're going to feel lost," he said Sunday night. "You're going to feel like you don't belong. Just stay mentally tough."

I walked down to Shilshole High with Drew, but that didn't help because he was as nervous as I was. We had trouble finding the locker room, and once we found it, we were afraid to ask where to get our equipment. Some of the players looked about twenty times bigger than the biggest guy we'd faced. A few had beards; more had piercings; almost all had tattoos. It wasn't a little jump we were taking; it was a huge jump. I was so nervous that I must have seen DeShawn Free six times before I registered who he was. "Good luck," I said to him. He nodded back but didn't say a word.

Brad Middleton, the guy who'd clued us in about Trahane, came over. "I thought both you guys would be here," he said, a big smile on his face. "Let me show you where you get your stuff."

I thought I'd feel better once I stepped onto the field, but I didn't. I'd listen intently to every single word Downs or any of the assistant coaches said, but not one would actually penetrate. That whole first day of practice, I was ten seconds behind everybody in everything. I butchered simple drills such as running through the tires and hitting the blocking sleds—drills I'd done a thousand times. My hands were like stones; it seemed as if I dropped every single pitchout that came my way. Five other guys besides me were trying out for running back, and I was last in everything. By five o'clock it was so bad that I went light in the head and was afraid I was going to faint, and I thought that would be the end of it, that I'd never be able to return. But somehow, some way, I got through the practice.

I'd seen Drew off and on during those two hours, but for most of the practice we were in different groups. When I met up with him afterward, he had his head down. "I sucked," he said. "And you know what the worst thing is? I'm going to go home and my dad will tell me that it's perfectly okay if I'm on JV, that the important thing is that I have fun. At least you won't have to listen to that."

He was right about that. My dad drank his coffee while I ate breakfast Tuesday morning. I told him most of what had gone wrong, but not all. "Nothing to worry about," he said. "Put yesterday out of your mind and start fresh this afternoon. A bad first practice is pretty typical and your coach knows it, but you can't string a bunch of them together. You've got to show him you belong."

I must have looked as down as I felt. How could I show the coach I belonged when I didn't think I did? My dad took another sip of coffee. "Let's get you a plan, Mick. Something specific. How many running backs were there?"

"Six," I said.

"Downs will probably carry three running backs,

maybe four. To be safe you've got to work yourself up to number three. Today, look for the weakest guy in the group. Stand next to him every time you can. Try to do all your individual drills just before or just after him. Who's the number one guy, the starter?"

"Matt Drager."

"Don't ever follow him; let somebody else eat his dust. Once you're sure the coach knows you're better than the number six guy, do the same thing to number five. Pick them off, like ducks in a row. One at a time ... boom, boom, boom. You've got three weeks to get ahead of three guys. You can do it."

Everything was easier the second day. We got our gear right away and were out on the field early. When we broke into groups by position, I steered clear of Matt Drager. The other guys, they were the ones I had to beat, starting with Nathan Dorsey. On Tuesday I worked it so that I was side by side with Dorsey as much as possible. I didn't worry about anybody but him. With my focus narrowed, most of the panic was gone. I just played. By Thursday I was sure the coaches knew I was better than Dorsey, so then I went after Aaron Cunningham, making sure we were shoulder to shoulder all practice long.

Friday after practice Coach Downs posted the depth charts for the first time. Drew was number three at quarterback; I was number four among the running backs. There was a chance we were in already, and we both knew it. But we couldn't let ourselves slip back one spot, and the best way not to slip is to push forward.

The guys we passed, they didn't like us at all. They'd glower at us in the locker room and trash-talk us, saying how we were punk eighth-graders and they'd take care of us yet. But you can't back down just because somebody is older than you, and we didn't.

After the last practice, two sheets of paper were posted outside the gym. Before he'd let us look, Downs called us together. "Those lists over there—one says varsity and the other says junior varsity. But don't go thinking that any of this is set in stone. You guys on JV—if you play well and some varsity player is dogging it, I'll bring you up in a heartbeat." He paused. "All right, then. I'm not having any mad dash over there. Juniors, you go first. Find your name and your name only, then go into the locker room."

We were last—Drew and me and DeShawn and a couple of other guys from different middle schools. I ran my hand down the varsity list and saw my name. I kept looking, even though I wasn't supposed to, and there was Drew's.

"I can't find my name on either list," DeShawn said, panicked.

"You're there." Drew pointed, shoving him and laughing. "Varsity. We all made varsity."

I called my dad as soon as I got home. "I knew it," he said. "I knew it. Where do you stand, number two or number three?"

"He didn't post depth charts. Just rosters."

"Come on, Mick. You know damn well where you stand."

He was right. I'd passed them all, except for Drager.

He went silent for a moment when I told him. "Can you get him?" he asked.

"I don't know," I said. "Maybe."

My mom came home about an hour later. She kissed me on the forehead and told me how happy she was for me. "Did you call your dad?"

"Yeah."

"I'm glad you did," she said.

5

EVERY DAY THAT SUMMER Drew and I were on the field at Shilshole High by nine in the morning. Coach Downs couldn't supervise practices—that was against league rules—but he left equipment on the practice field. We'd hit the blocking sleds, run through tires—all the regular stuff. After that, Drew would practice his passing. I couldn't sprint nonstop for hours, but we figured out ways to work on his timing. Then it was my turn. We'd practice handoffs and pitchouts, screen passes and passes into the flat. Two hours—that was our goal, and most days we made it. DeShawn came about half the time, and other guys would show for a week or two and then not return.

From eleven until three, we hung out together—his house, my house, along Market Street, on the beach by Golden Gardens—it didn't matter. We'd eat lunch, play some foosball or video games, and then head over to Crown Hill Park. Almost every day there were enough guys to get a flag football game going. The only thing we let slide was weightlifting. The weight room at Shilshole was closed down. The community center had a weight room, but it cost two dollars a visit and all the guys in there were old men. We tried it once in mid-July. It was a hot day, and most of the old guys had their shirts off. They looked saggy and disgusting. We never went back.

. . .

"How good do you think Drager really is?" I asked Drew one day while we were walking to my house from Shilshole.

"Pretty damn good," he said. "He's big and strong and fast. He's like a man, too. I bet he shaves every day."

"Do you think he's better than I am?"

He tilted his head back and forth. "You're quicker and you've got great hands, but he's tough to bring down. There's something scary about the guy. All in all I'd say you're almost even." He paused. "What about me with Clark?"

"Pretty much the same thing."

We walked for a while, both of us thinking.

Drew spoke first. "The thing is, both of them have got lousy attitudes. Downs doesn't like either one."

"Yeah, but Downs isn't going to make us starters just because he likes us."

. .

I got my driver's permit in late June. I was embarrassed to get it, because Drew and DeShawn were both a year away. But once I saw how jealous they were, it was okay. A couple of times a week, my mom would take me out in her Honda and we'd drive around the neighborhood. That was fun in the beginning, but by August it was boring. I wanted to drive the Jeep, but my dad insisted I get really good with the Honda first. "When your mom says you're ready, then I'll teach you how to work a clutch."

6

THAT WEEK WE WERE ALLOWED to start official practices. Downs had us doing two-a-days right from the start: a morning session in full pads with full contact, and an afternoon session in shorts and helmet. Drager and Clark were both on the first team; Drew and I were the backups. Not bad, considering how far down we'd started, but not where either one of us wanted to end up.

Taking the starting spot from Drager was going to be hard. The guy was a tough inside runner. I never saw him knocked backwards, not even by blitzing linebackers. He always delivered at least as good a hit as he received, and when he went down he got the extra yards that come with falling forward.

That wasn't true of me. Lots of times I got stopped right in my tracks and was unable to fall forward. So he had me on that. But on the sweep plays and on swing passes, I was able to get off and running just a split second faster. That split second meant that I could make the corner more often, and it meant that I had the better chance to break the big one.

That's exactly what I did one Friday on the last play of practice. We were running a seven-on-seven game.

Drager had pulled himself off the field, claiming some sort of injury, so I was working with the first team. Everybody else was dragging, waiting for practice to end, but the adrenaline was flowing for me. I took a pitchout from Aaron Clark and flat-out beat everybody to the corner. Once I was around it, I was off to the races. There's no feeling in the world like looking up and seeing green in front of you—green and green and more green. I streaked all the way into the end zone, untouched.

I trotted back, breathing heavily. Downs called for the ball and I flipped it to him. "Good effort, Johnson," he said. Then he turned on Drager. "Did you see how he got around the corner? No hesitancy. None. That's what I've been trying to get you to do for two years now." Drager didn't blink. But when Downs turned away from him, his eyes went straight to me. He stared me down for a while, and then he spit.

Downs blew his whistle, his assistants blew theirs, and two minutes later we were all on one knee, looking at him. "Monday morning, you'll find depth charts posted on the gym door. If you were a starter last year, you might want to check. I suspect some of you will be surprised. You give me effort, I'll reward you. You don't, I won't."

As I headed toward the locker room, Downs's eyes

caught mine and he gave me a nod. Was he telling me that I'd moved past Drager, that I was first team?

Back home, I took a long shower and ate, and then Drew came over. He'd seen my run for a touchdown and he'd heard Downs. "He was talking to you, Mick. No doubt about it. You wait. You'll be first team on Monday."

"I don't know," I said.

"Bet?"

I shook my head. "I don't want to jinx myself." We watched an Arnold Schwarzenegger movie and played some Madden NFL, and then he went home. Just after he left, my dad came in the door. Seeing him got my juices going again.

"How'd the week go?" he asked.

"Good," I said.

"Meaning?"

I couldn't keep it in. "Meaning I think I'm first team."

My dad's face broke into a huge grin. "That's it, Mick. That's the prize. Being a four-year letterman is good; being a four-year starter is ten times better."

. . .

When Drew and I neared the field Monday morning, a bunch of the guys were already grouped around the depth charts. I tried to act casual, and so did Drew. We walked up as if we were checking on the library schedule. I found the running back list and read the names: "1. Matt Drager, 2. Mick Johnson, 3. Curt Belfair."

"I'm still number two," Drew said to me, his voice low. "How about you?"

"Same," I said, my throat tight.

I felt somebody leaning on me. I turned: it was Drager.

"You're clueless, aren't you?"

"What are you talking about?" I said.

"What am I talking about? All that ass kissing you did last week, paying attention to every little thing Downs says and going full speed in every little drill he runs—it's a waste of time."

"Oh, yeah?" I said. "Why's that?"

He pushed his face right in to mine. "Downs doesn't start freshmen. Freshmen do the dirty work—punt returns and kick returns, all that special teams crap. It's his way of breaking you in. So stop looking at the board—your name is never going to be above mine. Number two you are, and number two you will remain."

I looked around. Brad Middleton had heard, and he nodded. "He's right, Mick. Unless Drager blows out his knee or something, you'll be lucky to get ten carries all year."

Drager grinned. "And I ain't getting hurt, Mick. So stop with all the rah-rah stuff. It makes everybody want to puke."

I wouldn't let myself believe it. All through the second week I outplayed Drager: I outhustled him, I outhit him. All through the second week Drager smirked at me. It drove me crazy, that smirk. He couldn't be right. He just couldn't.

But the next Monday, when Drew and I checked the depth charts, nothing had changed. "1. Matt Drager, 2. Mick Johnson."

"Let it go, Mick," Drew said to me at the end of the day.

"Let what go?" I said.

"Downs won't start us," he said. "We're going to have to wait our turn."

I looked at him. "Wait our turn? Drager's a junior, Drew. So is Clark. You're talking about waiting for two years."

He opened his hands in front of him. "There's nothing we can do." He was right and I knew it. But just thinking about telling my dad made my palms go cold.

That night I slipped downstairs once I heard the Jeep pull into the driveway. It was almost midnight. "Dad," I said as he opened the door.

He jumped. "Damn it, Mick, you startled me."

"I'm sorry. It's just that—"

"Give me a second, all right?" He put his briefcase down and went into the kitchen. I followed. He opened the refrigerator and got himself a beer. "All right," he said, once he'd opened it. "What's up?"

I took a deep breath and then explained Downs's policy and how he'd stuck to it for years. "I'll play on all the special teams, though. Kickoffs, punts, extra points, and field goals—I'm on every unit. It's not like I won't be out there."

He took a swig of his beer. "What about alternating? Any chance you and this Drager will do that?"

"No," I said. "I might get some carries in the fourth quarter of blowouts, but that's it."

He scowled. "That's stupid. It makes you sit there and hope your teammate breaks his neck."

"I know, but there's nothing I can do."

He put his beer down. "Mick, here's what I say: Keep outworking that Drager kid. Outwork him every damn day in every damn drill. Make that son of a bitch coach play you."

1

I ENDED UP practicing hard every single day, just like my dad wanted, but I wasn't doing it because I thought I had a chance to start. I was doing it because I didn't know how else to play. If the ball was in my hands, I was going to take it as far upfield as I could, and it didn't matter that it was only practice. Football was in my blood.

During the games, I was on the field only for kick-offs, punts, and extra points. But on those few downs, I played like a crazy man, flying down the field, breaking through blockers, and laying big hits on guys on the other team. In the opener, I blocked a field goal. And in the next three games I forced two fumbles, both of which led to touchdowns.

After those big plays, I automatically looked up into the stands toward the fifty-yard line to where my dad always sat. But he skipped those games; if I wasn't going to carry the ball, he wasn't going to show up.

. . .

After a Monday practice halfway through the season, Downs asked me to stop by his office. "Don't worry," he said. "It's all good."

Drew had overheard. "What's up?" he said.

I shrugged. "No idea."

I dressed quickly and then went to the coaches' office and knocked. He looked through the glass window and waved me in. "Sit down," he said, pointing to the chair.

He picked up a pencil and tapped it on his desk blotter. "I've noticed, Mick. From the first practice last spring to today, your hustle, your attitude—fantastic. Like no other kid I've ever coached. Ever. I've never had a freshman as a captain, not in ten years of coaching, but starting with our next game, there will be a 'C' on your helmet and a 'C' stitched on the right shoulder of your jersey." He stood and reached his hand across the desk. "Congratulations."

My face reddened with pleasure. "Thanks, Coach," I said. "Thanks a lot."

He smiled, his eyes alive. "It's not a gift. You earned it."

When I returned to the locker room, Drew came over. "So?"

I couldn't hide the smile taking over my face. "Downs made me special teams captain."

Drew didn't hold back. "Captain," he said, and then he pounded me a couple of times on the shoulder. "Good for you! Good for you!" He grabbed DeShawn Free. "Mick's just been made captain." DeShawn high-fived me, and then Drew went and grabbed another guy and another guy and another guy.

I told my mom when she came home from work. "Way to go." she said. "That is some honor." She paused. "Call your dad."

"I'll tell him when he comes home," I said.

"You'll be asleep when he comes home. Call and tell him now."

I dialed the station. "Your dad's on the air right now," a woman said. "But we break for a commercial in two minutes. Can you wait?"

Two minutes later his voice was on the line. "What's up?"

I took a deep breath. "Coach named me captain of the special teams. I'm the only freshman he's ever made captain, and he's been coaching for ten years. I get a 'C' on my helmet and the shoulder of my jersey."

"Hey, hey, hey," he said.

"Next game I make the call on the coin toss, and if there's any argument about penalties or anything like that on a kickoff or punt, I'm the one who goes to the ref."

"Wonderful." There was a pause. "How about playing time at running back? Now that you're captain, is that coach finally going to let you have some carries?"

His words sucked everything good out of me.

"You know how that works," I said. "Nothing's changed."

"What do you mean, nothing has changed? You're a captain now. Did you tell him you want to start?"

"I don't have to tell him, Dad. He knows."

"Mick, the 'C' on the uniform and on the helmet, that's all nice. But you're not going to make a name for yourself calling heads or tails." He paused. "Look, the commercial break is ending. I've got to get back to work. But go to your coach tomorrow. Tell him that if you're good enough to be captain, you're good enough to carry the ball."

I swallowed. "Dad—"

"Do it, Mick. You've got nothing to lose."

For the rest of the night and the next day, I kept thinking about what my dad had said. Sometimes it seemed as if he were asking me to slit my own throat, but at other times I'd think he was right. If Downs could make me a captain, why couldn't he let me start? And what did I have to lose? If he said no . . . so what?

After Tuesday's practice I walked down the long hallway and knocked on Coach Downs's office door. He looked up, motioned me in, and then picked up my game jersey from his desktop. A big "C" was on the right shoulder. "I was just going to send for you. Pretty cool, isn't it?"

"It's great," I said, fingering it. "Coach," I said.

"What?"

"I was just wondering if maybe I could get some carries at running back. Not start, but maybe alternate. I think I—"

"Stop right there, Mick."

"It's just that—"

"I said stop." He stared at me for what seemed like an hour. "I decide who plays and who doesn't, just like I decide who is captain and who isn't. You got that?"

I nodded.

"Okay, then. Now take your jersey and get out of here."

8

LITTLE BY LITTLE, the season slipped away. Eastlake had beaten us 28–16 in the opener, but after that we'd managed to sneak by everybody else we'd played. Some games we were the better team: Garfield and Franklin and Roosevelt had half the guys and half the talent. Some games we were lucky: Bothell fumbled five times in the first half. Woodinville's all-league quarterback was out with an injury, and his replacement threw three interceptions.

I was still playing hard on special teams, but I didn't even think about starting. After the whole captain thing, even my dad gave up. "Next year," I told myself. "Next year." And then I caught a break, and so did Drew. On the Sunday before the showdown with Foothill, the cops caught Drager and Clark drinking at Salmon Bay Park. They'd scuffled with the police and had ended up being handcuffed and dragged off to juvenile hall.

In school, kids talked about nothing else. Before Monday's practice began, Downs called the team together. He said the normal stuff about responsibility and maturity and then he told us that Drager and Clark had let the team down. "Look what a six-pack of beer cost them. They'll miss the Foothill game, the chance to win the KingCo title and move into the playoffs. Think hard before you act, because what you do carries consequences."

On the field, Downs moved Drew and me to the first team, which I expected. But since Drew had practiced more with DeShawn Free than he had with any other receiver, Downs decided to make DeShawn a starter too. It was as if we'd won the lottery. The workout was light—helmets and shorts—and through it all the offense was completely out of sync. But not even a bad practice could bring the three of us down. We were starting on Friday against Foothill. That was all that mattered.

I thought about staying up to tell my dad I was going to start against Foothill, or maybe writing him a note, but in the end I didn't. I decided it was smarter to wait until I was dead sure. There was always the chance that Drager would somehow weasel his way back onto the team and back into the starting lineup.

Tuesday and Wednesday came and went with no change. Thursday Clark and Drager were back at school. I stood off to the side and listened as Nolan Brown asked them how they stood. "We're done for the year," Drager said, his dark eyes glowering. "Even if you guys somehow beat Foothill, we won't play in the regionals. It sucks."

That night I waited up for my dad. As soon as I heard him come in the door, I slipped downstairs. "Hey, what's up?" he said.

"Can you get tomorrow night off?" I asked him.

He shrugged. "I don't know. I suppose. Why?"

"I'm starting," I said. "Against Foothill. The championship game."

9

OUR GAME DAY PRACTICES weren't really practices at all. Friday after school we met in the gym, did some stretching, a little running, and some more stretching. It was all over in forty-five minutes.

When I got home, I forced myself to eat half of the ham and cheese sandwich my mom had made for my pregame meal. Once I'd finished, I went upstairs and lay down, trying to rest. I kept opening my eyes, looking at the clock, hoping it was time to go. Every minute seemed like ten. It was an away game, over in Bellevue, and Downs was requiring that we go as a team on a school bus. We were to be in the school parking lot by six; Drew's dad was picking me up at five-fifty.

At last I heard a horn sound in the driveway. I grabbed my duffel, hustled down the stairs, and got in Drew's car. Forty-five minutes later I was stepping down off the school bus and heading to the locker room at Foothill High.

Once we were in uniform, Coach Downs told us we had to stay within ourselves, to play under control. My mind was racing so fast, I had to suck in air to calm myself down. Felipe Perez, one of the linemen, looked over at me and shook his head. "Save some energy,

Johnson," he said. "You're going to be worn out before the game starts."

As game time neared, a sense of power filled me. It started in the back of my head and spread like a wildfire until I felt as if I were going to explode. Right then Lee Choi went to a locker and started pounding on it, pounding and screaming. Nobody had ever done anything like that before any of our other games. I looked at Choi, and then I started pounding on the locker in front of me, pounding on it like one of those insane Norwegian berserkers I'd read about in sixth grade. I spotted Drew. I could feel him holding back. Then a little smile came to his eyes and he went over to a locker and started pounding and screaming, and then Brad Middleton, the middle linebacker, joined us, and after that Heath Swenson started up, and soon everybody was pounding on the lockers and screaming, getting higher and higher. After a couple of minutes, Coach Downs put his fingers in his mouth and blasted out one of those ear-piercing whistles of his. "All right, gentlemen," he hollered. "Let's play football."

We raced through the tunnel and onto the field. As I did my jumping jacks and sit-ups, I stole peeks up into the stands. My dad had told me he was doing half his shift to keep Lion happy but that he'd be in the stands by game time. I didn't see him for a while, but then I picked him out, and I got a rush that was like scoring a touchdown in the fourth quarter of a tie game. A little later a horn sounded, and then the Foothill band played "The Star-Spangled Banner."

Game time.

10

YOU CAN SCREAM all you want, but if you don't back it up on the field, it's just screaming.

Foothill High was unbeaten; they'd crushed teams that we'd barely sneaked by. On Thursday, Coach Downs had shown us films of the game from the year before. Drager's longest run had been eight yards, and by the end of the game you could see in his body language that they'd beaten him.

I wasn't going to let that happen. No matter how many times they pounded me into the ground, I wasn't quitting. "You never know when you might get a chance to break a long run," my dad had told me many times. "Always be ready."

We won the coin toss and received the kickoff. Michael Tucker, a senior cornerback, ran it out to the twenty-seven, and then Drew and I trotted out onto the field, starters for the first time. He looked at me, his eyes lit up like Christmas. "Here we go, Mick," he whispered.

Our first play was a power toss right. Drew's pitch was too slow, forcing me to break stride, which is why two Foothill players were waiting for me at the corner. I lowered my shoulder and drove into the first guy, but he held on until the second tackler brought me down. I gained two yards, maybe three. On second down I went straight up the middle with pretty much the same re-sult. That set up third down and five for a first down. Drew threw a quick slant right on the money to our tight end. Bo Jones caught it but was tackled a yard short of the first down, forcing a punt.

On the sidelines, I told myself to be patient. Two run-ning plays don't make a game—I knew that. I'd break a decent run on the next series. All I needed was for the offensive line to give me a sliver of daylight.

Foothill managed a couple of first downs but then got nailed for a holding penalty and punted the ball back. On first down, I ran a sweep left. When the blocking broke down, I reversed field, hoping to catch Foothill overpursuing, but their defensive end had stayed home. He wrapped me up around the knees and dropped me for a ten-yard loss. After that Drew threw a couple of dink passes that gained six yards and we had to punt again. Coming off the field, I kept my head up. Games are won and lost in your mind as much as on the field.

Both defenses dominated throughout the first quarter and into the second, but just before halftime, Foothill marched down the field as if they were playing a middle school team. Everything that hadn't been working for them—slant passes, draws, screens—suddenly worked. It made no sense, but sometimes football is a crazy game. The Foothill quarterback took the ball into the end zone untouched on a bootleg from the eight-yard line—our defense had fallen for a fake to the tailback. Foothill's kicker missed the extra point, so at the break we were down six.

In the locker room, Downs said the right things: how one touchdown was nothing, how we just had to keep fighting and things would go our way. The important thing was to stick to the game plan.

That's what he said, but it's not what he did. All through the first half, he'd had me run the ball. I hadn't gained much yardage, but I could feel their defense wearing down. Soon I'd break a big one. But instead of sticking with the running game, Downs called for three passes to open the second half: a screen that gained a yard; a long bomb to DeShawn Free that fell incomplete; and a slant that was nearly intercepted. We had to punt again.

The defense held Foothill to one first down, but our possession went like this: incomplete pass, incomplete pass, incomplete pass, punt.

Downs had given up on the running game, had given up on me, but Drew hadn't. "The draw play should be open," he said as we stood on the sidelines, waiting for another chance. "I'm going to call it next series, no matter what Downs sends in, so be ready." A freshman quarterback making his first start changing a coach's play—that took guts.

On our next possession, Drew threw two more passes, completing one, setting up third and five. We'd thrown on eight straight plays, and Downs sent in a ninth. "They're going to be blitzing," Drew said. "We'll run the draw."

"You changing the play?" Perez said.

Drew nodded. "I'm changing the play."

Perez looked around at the other linemen. "Let's block this sucker."

And they did. When I took the handoff, a huge hole opened right in front of me. In two strides I was past the linemen and the blitzing linebackers and was into the secondary. The strong safety came up and tried to tackle me high, but I fought him off. I cut left and juked the cornerback, and suddenly I was looking at seventy yards of empty space. The same feeling came to me that always comes when I break a long one. It was as if I were four years old again, out in my backyard, the little mini football cradled in my arm, the green grass underfoot, and the end zone straight ahead. I tucked the ball tightly against my side and took off straight for the goal line, my legs churning up the yards.

At the Foothill twenty, someone dived for my ankles and caught my heel. I stumbled a little, almost went down, but then righted myself, and seconds later I was in the end zone. I didn't spike the ball—that's a fifteen-yard penalty in KingCo. Instead, I ran to our sideline, took my helmet off, and raised it to the section where my dad was sitting. He was on his feet, pumping his fist and cheering, as our kicker, K. J. Solomon, split the uprights with the extra point, putting us ahead 7–6.

Our lead held throughout the third quarter and into the fourth. Downs had me running the ball again to eat up time. I'd pop free for a first down now and again, but we couldn't sustain anything. When Foothill had the ball, they'd march twenty or thirty yards, but then

something—a penalty, a dropped pass, a missed block—
would stop them. I remember looking up at the clock
in the fourth quarter. Still 7–6, with six minutes and
thirty-two seconds left. Was my touchdown run in the
third quarter going to be enough to win it?

After a short Foothill punt, I carried the ball twice,
gaining seven yards and setting up a third and three
near midfield. Downs called for a quick out pass to
DeShawn Free on three.

DeShawn must have thought it was on four, because
he was late getting off the line of scrimmage, forcing
Drew to hold the ball longer than he should have. Just
as he stepped up to throw, Foothill's middle linebacker
blind-sided him, jarring the ball free. It bounded crazily
along the ground for five yards or so until one of Foothill's big linemen, number 73, scooped it up. He was
slow, but he had a ten-yard lead and only fifty yards to
run. He rumbled down the field, gasping for air, looking
over his shoulder every five yards. I was closing on him
with every stride, but I never caught him.

Our lead was gone.

Worse, when I looked upfield, I saw Drew flat on the
ground. Guys were standing over him and our trainer,
an old guy named Mr. Stimes, was kneeling next to
him. By the time I reached him, Drew was up, but he

was clutching his right elbow, fighting the pain.

Foothill hit the extra point, making the score 13–7. As they lined up to kick off, Coach Downs called me over. "Drew won't be able to get any zip on the ball, not with that elbow."

"Feed me the ball," I said. "I can win it for us."

I could see his mind working. Then he nodded. "Let's see what you've got."

He walked away, and suddenly my legs felt like they weighed one hundred pounds each. I was tired, sore, beat up. Then I thought of the stakes: the league title, the spot in the playoffs. I thought of all the teams I'd played on, all the clinics and camps I'd gone to, all the hours and hours of practice beginning when I was four. It was for this. All that work was for this.

Tucker brought the kickoff straight up the field to the thirty-eight yard line, giving us good field position. Foothill figured we'd be passing, so they were playing their linebackers deep and their safeties even deeper, making it a perfect time to run. On first down, I drove the ball off right tackle on the stretch play. Foothill's outside linebacker tripped, and their safety was late coming up, so I picked up twelve yards before I was gang-tackled.

Two minutes and forty-eight seconds.

We went without a huddle. Their linebackers and

safeties were still playing deep. This time we ran the draw. Once I got past the linemen, I had eight free yards before I was dragged down at their forty.

Two thirty left in the game, clock running.

Foothill came up tight in their standard defense. They were done worrying about the pass; they were looking for me. I gained four yards on a toss sweep. Two minutes and two seconds left. I took a handoff straight up the middle for eight yards, running right through an outside linebacker, setting up a first down on the twenty-seven. One forty.

Foothill put eight guys in the box, daring Drew to throw. I was supposed to carry the ball over left tackle, but there was no hole. I stumbled against one of my own linemen, bounced off him, then reversed direction and headed to the right. Somebody—maybe DeShawn—laid a great block on the one Foothill guy who had a clear shot at me. I looked up and saw an open field. If only I could have made my legs move faster. Just across the ten-yard line a Foothill player tracked me down. When I hit the turf, I landed smack on top of the ball, knocking the wind out of me. For a long second I just lay there. But the clock . . . and with it the game . . . was ticking away. I forced myself back to the huddle.

The line judge raced to the hash mark and laid the

ball down. The guys lined up, Drew took the snap, and he immediately spiked the ball to stop the clock.

Second and goal on the eight-yard line.

Sixty-nine seconds left.

Downs sent in three plays so we wouldn't waste time huddling up. All three were for me. A draw play and two sweeps—the first right and the second left.

I sucked in air. We broke the huddle and I took my position.

"Hut! Hut!"

Drew dropped back as if to pass, then slipped me the ball. It was the play I'd scored on earlier, but this time the Foothill linebackers didn't bite. I was lucky to fight my way back to the line of scrimmage before I went down.

Third and goal from the eight.

Fifty-six . . . fifty-five . . . fifty-four.

Hurriedly, we lined up. As Drew took the snap, I broke for the outside. I watched the ball into my hands, squared my shoulders, and turned upfield, my eyes on the end zone. I thought I'd make it, even as I saw their safety close on me. I lowered my shoulder and hit him at the five. He wrapped his arms around me and pulled me down, but not before I'd fallen forward two more yards.

Fourth and goal from the three-yard line.

Thirty-four . . . thirty-three . . . thirty-two . . .

We had enough time; we'd get the play off. Three yards—that's all I needed. Three yards.

Everything slowed. I remember seeing the faces of the fans in the end zone, knowing that they were screaming but somehow not hearing them. "Hut!" Drew called, and I heard that. The center snapped the ball and I broke left. I caught Drew's pitchout in stride, my eyes on the end zone—it was so close I could taste it.

I saw number 50, Foothill's best linebacker, shed his blocker; I felt him hit me. All I had to do was keep driving with my legs and they'd carry me forward. It was just him and me, and there was no way one guy could bring me down, not with so much on the line.

That's when I felt the turf slipping out from under me. It was like being in a nightmare and wanting to scream but not being able to. I could feel myself going down, feel the ground rushing up at me. At the last instant, I reached the ball forward, trying to stretch over the goal line. I had to break the plane. I had to.

And then I was down. I looked at the ball, looked at my hands stretched out as far as I could reach.

I was twelve inches short.

11

FOOTHILL RAN a quarterback sneak, the final seconds ticked away, and then their guys started grinning and laughing and piling onto one another, celebrating their perfect season, their trip to the playoffs. I watched for a little—we all did—and then dragged myself into the locker room and changed into my street clothes. The whole time, I kept reliving those final seconds, kept feeling the turf give way. If only the field had been better. If only my spikes had been longer. The victory had been right there.

Finally I headed out. Downs had said that if we wanted, we could go home with a parent and skip the team bus. In the parking lot, I looked for my dad. Half of me hoped he hadn't waited, but he was there, standing by his Jeep. I got into the passenger seat. "You want to get something to eat somewhere?" he said.

I shook my head.

We drove over the Evergreen Bridge and took I-5 toward Green Lake. The whole way, neither of us spoke. When we reached Phinney Ridge, I broke the silence. "You saw what happened, didn't you?"

"I saw what happened."

"I mean with the turf. How the turf came out from under me? You saw that, right?"

He looked over, shaking his head. "Don't do it, Mick."

"Don't do what?"

"Don't go making excuses. That's BS. That's just total BS."

"I'm telling you what happened. I'm not making excuses."

"What happened is, the linebacker stopped you," he said. "What happened is, he was stronger. It was one-on-one, and he beat you. That's what happened." He took a breath and exhaled. "Look, Mick—it's okay to lose as long as you learn from it. So learn from it. You're close, but you're not there. You've got speed; you've got quickness; you've got knowledge of the game. More power in the red zone—that's the last thing."

I felt the anger rise, but I didn't answer.

When we got home, I showered and then climbed into bed. No way could I fall asleep, though. I let my eyes run over the posters on the wall. Walter Payton, Jim Brown, Eric Dickerson—the greatest of all time, and I had thought that someday I'd be one of them.

What a joke that was. With my teammates watching, with my dad watching, with every eye in the stadium on me, I'd failed. Completely and utterly failed. I'd been so sure of myself, so certain that if I got my chance, I'd make the most of it. How stupid! How like a third-grader! As if I were the only guy on the field with dreams. That linebacker who stopped me—number 50. Before the game he had probably dreamed of making the big hit to save the game for his team. So why did his dream come true and mine go up in flames? What had he done that I hadn't? Why had I failed? Why had I come up a foot short?

There was an answer. I tried to keep it from coming, but there was no holding it back. *You don't have the talent,* a voice whispered—my voice.

I looked at the posters on my walls, and I wanted to tear them all down and throw them away. It was as if the great running backs were on one side of a door and I was on the other, and the door had been slammed shut in my face, slammed shut and locked tight.

PART THREE

1

MONDAY I HUNG OUT with Drew and DeShawn at lunch and in between classes, and they kept telling me the loss to Foothill wasn't my fault. "It's just because your run was the last play that everybody remembers it," DeShawn said. "If it hadn't been for what you did earlier, we wouldn't have had a chance to win. Besides, did you see the arms on that guy who hit you? They were like my legs. I swear to God, he had to have been on steroids. I think half their guys were."

"You think so?" I said, looking first at DeShawn and then at Drew. "You think they were on steroids?"

Drew shrugged. "I don't know. You hate to call somebody a cheater without any proof, but some of those Foothill guys were just too damn big."

For the rest of the day, my mind kept going back and forth. Was number 50 a cheater? Were a bunch of them cheaters? Had they stolen the victory? Or was I being a poor loser by making excuses?

• • •

Toward the end of the day, a rumor started going around that Coach Downs was quitting. "Probably they'll blame that on us, too," Drew said, only half joking.

Downs was a PE teacher as well as head football coach, but he had a sub Tuesday and another one Wednesday, and both days he'd had meetings with the principal and the athletic director. Then on Thursday came the announcement: All football players were to attend a meeting after school.

At two-forty I went into the commons and pulled up a chair at a table where Drew and DeShawn were slouched, heads down. Our table was way in the back and in the far left corner, away from everybody. I looked over at Matt Drager and Aaron Clark. They were sitting front and center, right where we'd have been if I'd scored the winning touchdown.

Coach Downs came in at two-forty-five, accompanied by Hal Carlson, the custodian. Carlson, a burly black man, was a decent guy, but I had no clue why he'd be standing next to Downs, unless it was to chew us out about something going on in the locker room. About forty other guys were sitting at tables around us.

Downs strode to the front of the room and raised his

hand to settle everyone. "This is hard for me to say, so I'll just say it. I won't be coaching here next year. I've got an opportunity to become offensive coordinator at Pacific Lutheran, and I can't turn it down."

Downs let the murmuring go for a minute or two, and then he raised his hand again. "You guys have been great, and Shilshole High has been great. You're going to beat Foothill one of these years, go to the play-offs, and take it all. I know that, which makes leaving hard. Fortunately there is one thing I don't have to worry about. I know I'm leaving the program in good hands." He turned and looked at Hal. "Most of you know Mr. Carlson as the head custodian here. Starting today, he's also your head coach."

Guys looked at one another in shock. From the front table I heard Clark laugh out loud. "This is a joke, right?" Drager called out. "Hal's not really our—"

Downs started to answer. "This is no—"

Carlson cut him off. "Coach Downs, I'll handle the meeting from here."

Downs looked at him, pursed his lips, and then nodded. "You're right," he said. Then he turned back to us. "I'll be around school until the end of the semester. Stop by my office anytime you want."

He walked to the door, turned back again to wave, and then left. As soon as the door closed behind him,

Hal's eyes homed in on Drager. "Would you like to re-peat that question?"

Drager didn't back down. "I asked Coach Downs if he was joking."

"About me being the coach?"

"Yeah, about you being the head coach."

"You're Drager, right? And you're Clark?"

They both nodded.

"Running back and quarterback, right?"

Again they nodded.

"The kids who got arrested?"

The smiles disappeared.

"Well, Mr. Drager and Mr. Clark, I will be reviewing your case in the next few weeks to determine what your future status on this team will be. Once I've ac-quainted myself with the facts, I'll let you know whether I will allow you the privilege of playing foot-ball for Shilshole High next year. As of now, you remain suspended. Since this is a meeting for team members only, you will have to leave."

Aaron Clark laughed nervously. "Are you kicking us out?"

Carlson nodded. "I'm kicking you out."

Drager and Clark exchanged a look, smiled at each other and at their friends, then got up and left, slamming the door behind them. My eyes—everybody's eyes—had followed them on their way out. Once they were gone, we looked back to Carlson.

The fury was still in his eyes, but it was gone from his voice. "From now on, when you address me, you will call me Coach Carlson or Coach. As to team rules: there's only one word you need to remember, and that word is *respect*. Respect yourself, respect one another, and respect the game. Do that and you and I will get along fine. Don't"—he looked toward the door Drager and Clark had just slammed—"and you won't be playing for me." His eyes scanned the room. "All right then. Now I want to hear from you. We'll start with the guys at the table in the back. Tell me your name, your position, and your year in school."

One by one, players stood and gave the required information. Now and again Carlson would ask a question. "What do you bench-press?" Or "How fast do you run the forty?" Or "What's your vertical leap?"

It took time, but Carlson questioned every player. When he finished, he folded his arms across his chest. His forearms were huge—a lineman's forearms. "A week from Saturday, we're going down to Tacoma to watch the 4A championship game. I've arranged for a bus and I've got tickets for all of you. Attendance is required. You got a date with your girl, change it. And don't even ask me if you can bring her." With that, he turned and walked out.

Drew, DeShawn, and I left together. When we were clear of the other guys, Drew looked at me. "Wow!" he said.

"Do you think he'd really kick them off the team for good?" I said.

Drew shook his head. "He's just trying to scare them."

"I don't know about that," DeShawn said, smiling. "My money is on a suspension, which means you two sorry souls are going to get a second chance."

Drew turned to me and punched me a few times on the arm. "He might be right, Mick."

At school the next day, Brad Middleton told us that Carlson had once been head coach at Snohomish High. We went to the library during English class, which gave me a chance to go on the Internet to check it out. Snohomish High had a good Web page, so it was easy to find their head football coaches. Sure enough, there was Carlson's name. He'd been head coach for nine years. Every one of his teams had had winning records, and two of them had gone to the state playoffs. He'd coached his last team five years earlier, and they'd finished 7-3.

I stared at the screen, wondering why he'd quit. Maybe he burned out, or someone got sick in his family, or he hated the athletic director. Whatever the reason, Snohomish had gone straight downhill once he'd left. The bell sounded. I logged off, gathered my books, and headed toward my Spanish class. In the hallway, I spotted Coach Downs. "Good luck next year, Coach," I said.

"Hey, thanks, Mick," he said, and he fell in step with me. For a while neither of us spoke, but as I started down a side hall, he stopped me. "You know, Mick, you could be a terrific player. You've got great moves, great speed. You just need to bulk up a little, get stronger. Hit that weight room harder and there's no telling how far you can go."

"I will, Coach," I said.

He clapped me on the shoulder. "Good luck to you."

I hustled to get to class before Ms. Koss called roll, and just made it.

I hadn't paid much attention to what Downs had said; I figured he was just talking to talk. But as Spanish class crawled along, what he'd meant came home.

He was telling me I was weak. That's what it amounted to, when you cut through all the polite garbage. And that's what my dad had said, too, though I hadn't heard it that way. They were telling me that it wasn't enough to have moves and speed. In the red zone, in those final twenty yards, power was the name of the game. Not speed, not agility, not finesse. Raw power.

2

SATURDAY NIGHT was the state 4A title game. Drew wasn't crazy about going; I heard him and DeShawn complaining that they were going to miss some movie with Natalie Vick and her friends, but I wanted to see the game. My dad always said that you couldn't be the best until you knew what the best looked like.

And Pasco was the best. Early in the season they'd beaten Long Beach Poly, a powerhouse team from California, had gone undefeated through their league, and had defeated Foothill 20–16 the week before. Pasco had a running back named Ivan Leander who averaged ten yards every time he touched the ball.

I was the first player in the Shilshole High parking lot, but I wasn't there long before Middleton and Jones showed up, and then a bunch of other guys came. The last two were Drew and DeShawn. We were expecting a crummy yellow school bus, but a luxury Gray Line bus pulled into the parking lot. Even after the door opened with a hiss, nobody stepped inside. "Is this for us?" somebody called out to Carlson.

He turned and looked back at us. "Time to go, men."

Tacoma is thirty miles from Seattle, but with traffic the ride took an hour. Nobody much cared. Everybody was laughing and talking loudly, having a good time.

The Tacoma Dome holds twenty thousand and was about half full. Carlson had us sit as a team on the fifty-yard line high above the field. "You can see plays develop better from up here. Pick out the guy playing your position and watch him closely. He's who you want to be."

The Pasco players raced out of the tunnel first. As they ran they let out a wild man roar that grew louder and louder until it exploded into the word "Bulldogs." After that came a crazy howling as they crammed into an ever-narrowing circle and jumped all over one another.

A minute or two later, the Rogers players rushed onto the field. The noise that the Pasco fans had let loose worked like a challenge to the Rogers side. They stood and hollered louder and longer.

Pasco's warm-up routine was good, but Rogers's was amazing. Their coach blew his whistle and immediately the players rushed toward the goal line, formed a perfect circle with the captains in the middle, and started doing jumping jacks, sit-ups, pushups. Next came another whistle, and within seconds they had broken up into different subgroups, and each subgroup had a coach directing it. At the ten-yard line, two sets of linemen charged each other as a running back practiced hitting the holes. At the thirty, the quarterbacks took turns throwing to receivers. Along the sidelines, the punter kicked to the return men. By the end zone, the placekicker practiced field goals.

A horn sounded and both teams lined up at midfield. As the stadium announcer called out the name of each player, people cheered, but when the stars were announced, the roar would go up a dozen decibels. After the introductions came "The Star-Spangled Banner," and then finally the kickoff.

All through the first half, I wasn't quite sure what I was watching. It was supposed to be a game between the two best teams in the state, but Rogers seemed mediocre. They had only a handful of plays, and they ran them from the same formation: two backs, a wide out, and a receiver in the slot. Sometimes they'd send their fullback right up the middle; sometimes they'd run off tackle with the halfback; sometimes the slot receiver, coming in motion just before the ball was snapped, would take a handoff from the quarterback and go wide. They were incredibly crisp, just as you'd expect after watching their warm-ups, but the whole offense was simple.

On most of their possessions, Rogers made a first down or two, and then Pasco would stop them and they'd punt. They did have great special teams—time after time their punter would pound the ball down the field, and the cover team would pin Pasco deep in their own territory. But it didn't look as though Rogers could ever score.

When Pasco had the ball, the game kicked into high gear. Leander was like the Cheshire cat—now you see him, now you don't. Their quarterback didn't throw much, but when he did, he rifled the ball to his two wide receivers, both of whom had great hands. Pasco pushed Rogers around as if they were a JV team. Or at least, Pasco pushed them around until they got inside the twenty-yard line. But once they reached the red zone, something always seemed to go wrong. On the first drive it was a penalty for a block in the back, on the next drive Leander was hit so hard he coughed up the ball, on another there was an interception in the end zone. Pasco outgained Rogers four to one, but it wasn't until just before halftime that they finally pushed the ball into the end zone on a fourth and inches play, and even then no one was really sure Leander made it.

3

THROUGHOUT THE GAME, Carlson sat with one group of guys or another. He'd talk to them for a few minutes and then leave. At halftime, he came down and sat with us. I tensed up, and I could tell DeShawn and Drew did, too. "Tell me your names again," he said, "and your positions." When I told him my name, his eyebrows went up. "You're the freshman who got stopped a yard short on the last play against Foothill. I was at that game. Very exciting."

"A foot short," Drew said. "He was only a foot short."

He smiled wryly at Drew. "Okay. A foot." Then he paused before saying: "Short."

None of us spoke for a while. Carlson scratched the side of his face and then looked back to me. "So, who's going to win?" he said.

It was a no-brainer.

"Pasco," I answered.

"You boys think so, too?"

Drew and DeShawn nodded in agreement.

"You sure?"

"Pretty sure," DeShawn said. "They're ahead by six, and they could be ahead by twenty-six. I think they'll blow Rogers out."

Carlson nodded, then looked at Drew. "You're a quarterback, right?"

"Yes, sir."

"Okay, Mr. Quarterback. Tell me this. It's fourth and one. You've got the ball. Which defense scares you more: Pasco's or Rogers's?"

Drew laughed. "Fourth and one? Those Rogers guys are tough, that's for sure. I guess I'd rather go against Pasco."

Carlson stood. "Enjoy the second half, gentlemen." With that, he walked over to another group of guys.

"He actually thinks Rogers is going to win," DeShawn said. Then he shook his head. "What's he been smoking?"

I kept quiet. If I'd had to bet, I'd have picked Pasco. But something my dad said kept running through my mind: *Let a team hang around, and they'll end up beat-*

ing you. Pasco had definitely let Rogers hang around.

The third quarter seemed no different than the first two. Pasco kept piling up the yardage but would then self-destruct in the red zone. Rogers would squeeze out a first down or two, and out would come their incredible kicker. After the punt, Pasco would drive down the field again but never push it all the way into the end zone.

Near the end of the third quarter, Carlson came our way again. "Notice anything?" he said. We looked onto the field. None of us saw anything. "Check out the Pasco guys. They're all leaning forward; they've all got their hands on their knees, sucking air. Those guys are gassed." He paused while we looked. "Now look at the Rogers players. Standing tall, every last one of them."

Halfway into the fourth quarter, with the score still 6–0, Pasco had the ball near the fifty. On first down, the quarterback dropped back to pass. Rogers blitzed a safety; the Pasco fullback who was supposed to block him never saw him. The safety blind-sided the quarterback just as he started to pass. The ball floated like a party balloon toward the middle of the field. Rogers's cornerback cut in front of the intended receiver, plucked the ball out of the air, and took off. Fifty . . . forty . . . thirty . . . twenty . . . somebody dived at his feet but came up short . . . fifteen . . . ten . . . five . . .

Touchdown Rogers!

It was so unexpected that it took the Rogers fans a few seconds to start roaring, but once they started, you'd have sworn fifty thousand people were screaming. The placekicker split the uprights with the extra point, putting Rogers ahead 7–6.

With the lead, the Rogers guys were supercharged. They held Pasco on downs on the next possession, blowing through the line on each play. The Pasco punter got off a high spiraling punt that pinned Rogers back on their own twenty-yard line. A couple of running plays got Rogers nine yards, leaving them with a third down and one yard to go for a first down.

In similar spots all game long, Rogers had run the fullback on a dive into the line. This time the quarterback faked the handoff and dropped back to pass. From high above we could see the tight end come wide open in the middle of the field. The pass was perfectly thrown; the tight end caught the ball in stride at the forty-five yard line, and he was off to the races—no Pasco player came within ten yards of him.

Pasco had one final possession, but they had no life at all. On fourth and ten, their quarterback tossed the ball about five yards behind his intended receiver.

Rogers took over and ran out the clock. When the final horn sounded, DeShawn stood up. "You know something? Our new coach knows football."

4

A BUNCH OF THINGS HAPPENED over the Christmas break, most of them good, one of them strange, and the last one great.

I turned sixteen the day after school broke for the holidays. My mom took me to the department of licensing off Greenwood. During football season, I hadn't had much time to practice driving. Guys on the team had talked about how they'd flunked on their first try, so I was nervous, but I did okay with everything except parallel parking. At the end, the examiner handed me a sheet with the number 82 on top. "Congratulations," she said.

I drove the Honda home. When we were inside, my mom gave me a lecture on driving responsibly. She'd printed off the Internet a page with twenty safe-driving rules, and she had me sign at the bottom of the page. "Break any of these," she said, "and you lose your driving privileges. Understood?"

That next morning my dad came downstairs while I was eating breakfast. "I hear you passed your driving test," he said.

"First try."

"It took me three. I kept rolling through stop signs." He poured himself a cup of coffee. "You got anything planned for this morning?"

"I was going to call Drew."

"Don't. It's time I taught you how to drive the Jeep. That is, if you want to learn."

"You bet I want to learn."

"All right then. Finish your breakfast." He stopped and gave me one of those looks that let you know there's a joke that you're not in on. "I know the perfect place."

He took Fifteenth across the Ballard Bridge and turned toward Discovery Park. He wound along one of the wooded park roads for a while and then made a quick turn into a driveway and put on the brakes. "Okay, let's switch seats."

I looked up. In front of me were hundreds of tombstones. "This is a cemetery."

He laughed. "Like I said—the perfect place to learn."

It turned out he was right. There were no other cars, not one, so when I screwed up engaging the clutch and the Jeep lurched forward and then died—which happened a lot—nobody was behind me to honk. The roads in the cemetery meandered, turning this way and that, so I was constantly shifting back and forth from second to third to second. All through it were rolling hills that gave me a chance to practice engaging the clutch and working the emergency brake. It took a while, but after an hour I had the knack. "You're pretty good," my dad said when he took the wheel back. "A couple more times and you'll be ready to go on the road."

Then came the strange thing.

Instead of going home, my dad drove over to I-5. "Where we going?" I said.

"You'll see."

We went north to Mountlake Terrace, and he wound his way through a bunch of back roads. "There," he said, pointing to a billboard. GUN RANGE—FIRST TIMERS FREE! the sign promised. He followed a gravel road about half a mile before pulling into the parking lot. "You're sixteen," he said. "Time you learned how to fire a gun."

"A gun? What for?"

"It's something every man should know how to do."

We got out of the Jeep and walked across the parking lot. When my dad pushed open the door, little bells rang. A leathery-faced guy behind the counter was watching an NBA game on the television.

"What can I do for you?" he said.

"Is the first time really free?" my dad asked.

He laughed. "Not exactly. It'll end up costing you ten bucks. What do you want to shoot?"

"Not me. My son. I want him to learn how to shoot a gun."

"What size?"

"You got a little Colt he could use? A revolver?"

"Sure. You want to show him, or do you want me to?"

"I'd rather you did it," my dad said. "I'm no expert."

"That'll cost a little more."

"No problem."

The leathery guy turned to me. "Okay, son, this way."

We walked through a door to an indoor firing range. Before he did anything else, Bert Bronson—that was the name on the guy's shirt—gave me the rundown on gun safety. Then he nodded toward a target pinned up on the opposite wall and handed me a Colt revolver. "Let's see what kind of eye you got."

The whole thing had seemed like a joke until Bert handed me the gun. When I felt the cold metal in my hand, everything changed. It was small, not much bigger than my hand; still, it was a real gun with real bullets. You hold a gun, and you've got life or death in your hand.

I listened carefully as Bert gave me some tips on holding a gun and aiming it and on squeezing the trigger. "A little revolver like this doesn't have much recoil," he said, "but it takes some getting used to."

He was right. At first, the gun kept jumping in my hand, making me fire way high. But after a while I was able to hit the target, if not the bull's-eye. "Good enough," Bert Bronson said. "This isn't exactly a marksman's gun."

We walked back to the lobby area. The NBA game was over and my dad was sitting on a plastic chair, reading a newspaper. "That it?" he said.

"Not a whole lot to a little Colt," Bert said. "Kind of a squirt gun with a jolt. Now if you'd like him to learn how to handle a rifle, that's different."

"Another time," my dad said. He went to the counter and paid. "I appreciate your help."

"Don't mention the gun range to your mom," he said as he backed the Jeep up and returned to the road. "She wouldn't understand."

5

THE GREAT THING happened last.

Just before Christmas my Grandpa Leo and Grandma Harriet came, as usual. When Grandpa Leo found out that I had my driver's license, he shook his head back and forth. For the first time ever, they didn't insist on taking me to McDonald's, and I sure didn't mention miniature golf. Mainly they stayed in the living room, talking with my mother. Christmas Day, all five of us went to church.

My mom went to services every Sunday, but my dad went only on Christmas and Easter, and that's when I went. When we came back, I opened my presents. I got clothes, some books, a few gift cards from my mom, and two hundred dollars from Grandpa and Grandma. But I didn't get anything from my dad. He raised his index finger and mouthed the word "Later."

The day after Christmas Mom took my grandparents to the airport. "That wasn't so bad," she said when she returned.

"Leo is looking old," my father said.

My mom nodded. "I know. Mom says he's starting to forget things."

They fell silent for a moment. Then my dad turned to me.

"Do you like the Jeep, Mick?"

"Yeah, sure," I said. "It's great."

He took the Wrangler keys out of his pocket and laid them on the table. "Good, because it's yours. Merry Christmas."

"Are you serious?"

"Completely." He paused. "You'll have to work for me to pay for insurance and gas. I figure four hours a week ought to cover it."

I guess my mouth was hanging open in disbelief. My mom explained:

"Mick, Drew's dad has been driving you everywhere. We know he has. All right, there was nothing to be done. Your dad was working and I was working. But we are not going to take advantage of him for three more years. You've got your license, so it just makes sense, what with practices and games, for you to have your own car."

My dad nodded toward the keys lying on the table. "Go ahead. Take them. I suspect you'll want to go for a ride."

I went to pick them up, but my mother put her hand over mine and held it there. "The contract you signed—

everything in it still stands. You break any of those rules, and the Jeep comes back."

I nodded. "I know," I said.

"And I want to know where you're going, who you're going with, and when you'll be back every time you leave this house. And that cell phone stays on. Understood?"

"Yes," I said.

She let go. I picked the keys up from the table and headed for the door, so excited I was shaking. When I reached the door, I turned back to my dad. "What are you going to drive?"

"I'm buying a Dodge pickup from a guy at work. Very cool-looking, deep purple, oversize tires, lots of bells and whistles. He's bringing it by tonight. It'll help when we broadcast from outside the studio."

My mom held up one finger. "One hour, Mick. I want you home in one hour."

. .

I picked up Drew and then went to DeShawn's place and got him. They thought I was incredibly lucky to have my driver's license. I had to tell them the Jeep was mine over and over before they finally believed me. We drove around for a while and eventually ended up at

Carkeek Park. "Does this have four-wheel drive?" DeShawn asked.

"I think so," I said.

He pointed to Piper's Creek, the banks of which were visible from the parking lot. "If it's got four-wheel drive, you could drive right smack into that creek and come up on the other side."

We all stared at the creek for a bit. "Try it, Mick," Drew said.

"I'm not driving into any creek."

"Come on."

"It's not happening." I looked at my watch. "I told my mom I'd be back in an hour," I said. "She's pretty nervous about all this."

6

THE FIRST DAY BACK in January, weight training began. Thinking about working hard in the weight room—that's easy. Actually doing it, that's a whole different thing. I'd always figured weights were really important for linemen and linebackers but not so much for running backs. It was a mind-set I had to get out of, not just for one day, but for every day.

I stood outside the weight room with Drew and DeShawn. They were both talking about how much they hated lifting. Normally I would have joined right in with their whining, but now I couldn't let their attitude seep into me.

Guys filtered down in small groups. Some of them were eager—Middleton always loved lifting. But most of them had that dentist's office look on their faces. I kept waiting for Drager and Clark to show.

When Carlson arrived, he opened the door to the weight room and we trailed in behind him. Right away I could see changes he'd made. Banners with the words BIGGER, FASTER, STRONGER were plastered over all the walls. So were posters from the Super Bowl and the Rose Bowl and the Orange Bowl.

That wasn't the only change. As Carlson walked us through the room, you could tell how much thought he'd given to everything. The equipment was the same —an aging Smith machine and lots of free weights— but now it was arranged into stations all around the room. On the wall behind each station, Carlson had mounted photos showing what lift we were to do and how we were to do it. Below the photos was a clipboard where we were to write down the weight we'd lifted and the repetitions we'd done.

After he'd explained all the stations, Carlson faced us. "I heard Coach Downs in here every day barking at you guys. But I'm not checking on anybody. I've got my job to do out there in the school; you've got your job to do in here. I'll just say this. You saw Rogers; you saw Pasco. It was pretty exciting for them, playing for a championship, TV cameras rolling, stadium rocking, college recruiters watching every down. They played that game in December, but those guys got there because of the off-season work they did in the weight room. If you want to experience a championship, then you have to put in a champion's effort. Not one day—every day." He paused. "Last guy out turn off the lights."

Carlson left the weight room. We stood, looking around, unsure what to do. Middleton spoke up. "You heard the man. Let's get to it."

You need one guy to spot you during weightlifting. I let Drew and DeShawn work together and partnered up with Middleton. He was stronger than I was by a long shot, but with his easy smile and his easy ways, he didn't make any fuss about having to take weights off and put them back on. And seeing how much he lifted gave me still one more push.

I worked harder in the weight room than I ever had before. I was so focused on my workout that it wasn't until it was over that I realized Drager and Clark had never shown up.

"They quit the team," DeShawn said as we left.

"What?" I said.

"Laura Shelly told me this morning. Her older sister Kim is Clark's girlfriend. They're transferring to West Seattle. That's a triple-A school—we won't even play against them next year."

7

BY DINNERTIME, my shoulders and hamstrings had tightened. I took it as a good sign—I'd never gotten stiff from lifting before, which meant that I really had gone at it harder. I took a hot bath and then stretched out on my bed, punching buttons on the TV remote.

On one channel was one of those dumb infomercials peddling some health junk. I was about to switch to something else when this really ripped guy held up a bottle of pills and started talking about how they'd changed him from a ninety-pound weakling into a man-monster. The commercial showed before and after photos to prove it. They were crazy photos— probably of two different guys—but they got me thinking about the supplement stores out there. How could they stay in business if everything they sold was useless? I was committed to the weight room, one hundred percent. And I wasn't going to use steroids like number 50 and the other Foothill guys probably did. But if there were legal things out there that could make me stronger, it would be stupid not to take them.

Saturday morning I drove to the supplement store at University Village. I found an entire aisle filled with bottles promising muscle and weight gain. I floundered around until one of the clerks, a tall guy with a blond ponytail, came over. "You looking to bulk up?"

"I'm starting to lift weights seriously," I said, "and I was looking for—"

"You were looking for this," he said, holding up a bundled package of a protein powder with vitamin and mineral supplements. "You take all these and lift weights, and I promise you fantastic results."

I looked at the price on the package. "It's pretty expensive," I said.

"Nothing worthwhile is cheap," he answered.

That night I sat at my desk and worked the numbers. I had Christmas money from my grandparents and eight hundred dollars in the bank. That would pay for a six-month supply, but no more. Then I thought about all the clinics and camps my dad had paid for, all the equipment he'd bought me. They'd cost money. Well, this was for football, too.

My dad was out in the shed, cutting boards for new shelving. The table saw was screeching so loudly that it took a while to get his attention. Finally he shut the saw off, and I put a leaflet down in front of him. "What's this?" he said, taking his goggles off.

"You were right—I need more power, more strength. I'm going to work way harder at weight training this off-season. These are supposed to help."

He scanned the leaflet. "I drank a few protein shakes in my time. At Washington, the strength coach was all over us about nutrition." He handed the leaflet back to me. "Looks good, Mick. Take them." He started to put his goggles back on.

"I want to," I said quickly, "only . . ."

"Only what?"

"Only I don't have enough money."

He scratched the top of his head and smiled. "I get it. Okay, how much?"

"About one fifty a month."

He blew out softly. "Wow. That's a fair amount of money." He thought for a little while. "I'll tell you what. You're working four hours a week for the Jeep—that doesn't change. But if you want to work more hours, I'll pay you. You can start by helping me with this project. After that there's painting and cleaning the basement and a million other things. You find out what minimum wage is, and I'll pay two bucks more per hour. What do you say?"

I didn't have to think it over. "It's a deal."

I stuck my hand out and we shook.

Sunday morning I took down the old shelves in the shed. The work was gross—there were tons of spiders and spider webs in the corners. My dad rented a U-Haul truck, and I loaded up all the trash and took it to the transfer station. I started at seven and didn't finish until two. He counted out my pay and gave it to me on the spot.

After lunch, I drove to the supplement store and found the same clerk. I took the money my dad had paid me, added a chunk of my Christmas money, and bought four big bottles of pills and two bags of a powdery protein stuff that you added to milk. "You've also got to eat well," the clerk said as he bagged it. "Meat, dairy, fruits, vegetables, nuts, and beans. No junk. You stuff your body with French fries and drink Coke every day and none of this will do you any good."

. . .

The pills were easy, but the first sip of the protein powder made me gag. I pinched my nose as I swallowed down the rest, and it wasn't as bad. At dinner I told my mom that I was going to eat healthy. "Don't buy any more junk food," I said.

"Glad to hear it, Mick."

Only one thing bothered me: I had to drink a protein shake and take two pills at school during lunch. The clerk had said that timing was key. I was going to have to mix the protein powder into my milk, and Drew and DeShawn would razz me for sure. I decided to try to make a joke of the whole thing.

Sure enough, when I got a cup and added the powder to my milk on Monday, they both grimaced. "What's that?" Drew asked.

"It's a protein powder." I stirred. Most of the powder dissolved, but some yellow stuff floated on the top.

"Looks nasty-nasty," DeShawn said. "What's it supposed to do?"

"Make me bigger and stronger. You want to try it?" I said, pushing the milk toward him.

He shuddered. "No way, José."

I drank it down and then wiped my lips with the back of my hand. "Dee-licious." I flexed my biceps. "This stuff is going to turn me into the Hulk."

8

THE NEXT WEEKEND, my dad had me paint the upstairs computer room. I didn't mind doing the walls, but I hated the windows and the doors. I'd arranged to meet Drew and DeShawn at three on Sunday, and I had to hustle to finish.

I was getting set to carry the paint out to the shed when my dad came up to check on my work. He stood in the center of the room and looked at each wall, and then the ceiling. "Not bad," he said. "I'll move the furniture back."

"Thanks," I said, and I took a step toward the door.

"Wait a minute, Mick," he said. "I want to show you something."

I turned back, thinking he'd found a drip or a gob of paint on something, but instead he was sitting at my mom's desk, a small mahogany box in front of him. He motioned for me to come closer, and I did. "You ever notice this box?" he said, his face serious.

I shook my head.

"It's on the bottom shelf of the bookcase in the far left corner."

He opened it. Inside were a few two-dollar bills and a handful of foreign coins. He tipped the box over so that the coins and bills fell into his left hand. He put those on top of the desk.

"I'm out late every night now, Mick. And pretty soon I'll be going on trips for a week at a time. Ben Braun stayed in Seattle, but Lion Terry likes to take the show on the road. That means you and your mom are going to be alone more, which is why I'm showing you this." He pointed inside the box to a small button. "The box has a false bottom. Push the button."

"What's inside?"

"Push the button." I pushed the button and the bottom slid back.

In the hidden compartment was a gun.

"It's just like the one you fired at the range. There's a ninety-nine point nine percent chance you'll never need it, but I can't stand the thought of being away and having something go terribly wrong and having you and your mom here defenseless." He stopped. "I'm trusting you to be a man about this, Mick. You never touch it—ever—unless you feel threatened. No showing it to your friends, none of that."

"Is it loaded?"

"There's no point in having a gun unless it's loaded. Now I want your promise that you won't touch this unless you absolutely need to. Do I have it?"

I nodded.

"Say it."

"I promise," I said.

"Okay. One more thing. Not a word to your mom about this. She'd want it out of the house."

He put the gun in the box, then pushed the button, and the false bottom slid back, covering it. Next he returned the two-dollar bills and the coins. Finally he put the box in the bookcase, bottom left.

I brought the paint cans down to the shed, cleaned the brushes, and threw away the masking tape and the papers. After I locked up the shed, I stood a moment in the yard, thinking.

The Jeep, and now the gun. I wasn't a little kid anymore. I'd been saying that for a long time. But now my dad was saying it, too, and that was different. And a little scary.

9

I WAS SET. I had school, and I had weightlifting after school. I had the Jeep, and I had a way to make money. I was taking my protein and my supplements, and I was eating right. Matt Drager was off the team and was headed out of the school. I was getting along great with Drew and DeShawn, hanging out with them on Friday and Saturday nights, playing flag football with them on Saturday and Sunday afternoons. So when my dad told me about Popeye's the day before he left for Miami, I wasn't all that interested.

"The radio station just bought it," he said, his voice excited. "The fitness center in Fremont. You know the place I mean, don't you?"

"Yeah," I said, "I know the one you mean."

"I get a free membership with my job. And since you're my son, you get a free membership, too. You could do your weight training there."

"I don't need to; I lift with the team at school."

"Come on, Mick," he said. "Be serious. Popeye's is state of the art. What do you have at school? Some rusty old free weights and a couple of old Smith machines? Am I right?"

"Pretty much."

"Popeye's has a machine designed specifically for every muscle group. They've got cable stuff, dumbbells, barbells, ellipticals, treadmills, bicycles, medicine balls —everything. I can even get you some time with a personal trainer. That's not free, but I do get a discount. One hour at Popeye's would be like three hours at your school." He paused. "You said you wanted to get bigger, faster, stronger, right? Okay, here it is, an opportunity."

He was right. The equipment in the weight room at

school was old and there wasn't much of it. I spent too much time waiting and not enough time lifting. "It sounds good," I said. "Only . . ."

"Only what?"

"The other people there—they'd all be adults, right?"

He scowled. "Mick, you're sixteen; you're not a child."

"I know," I said.

He sighed. "Call Drew. He can be your guest the first time, and then after that we'll figure something out. Maybe you can pretend he's your brother, although with your red hair and his big ears, you two don't look alike. I'll arrange a trainer for next Saturday afternoon."

The next day I asked Drew. "That gym on the Burke-Gilman trail?" he said.

"Yeah."

He shook his head. "I don't know, Mick. I always figured that place was kind of gay."

"I know," I said, "but my dad really wants me to go. He's going to get us a personal trainer. One time, okay?"

I picked Drew up Saturday and drove to Fremont. I parked the Jeep in front of a red house on Canal Street and we walked along the waterfront trail to reach Popeye's. When we were twenty yards away, we could see shirtless guys working out in front of floor-to-ceiling plate-glass windows. "You sure about this?" Drew said.

"No, but we're here, so we might as well give it a try."

Inside the front door was a black semicircular counter. A musclebound guy, his head shaved bald, sat on a barstool, paging through a magazine, but he looked up the moment we walked in. "Can I help you?"

"I'm Mick Johnson," I said, suddenly afraid my dad hadn't called. "My father—"

"The guy on the radio at night," he said. "The guy who owns us."

"My dad doesn't own—"

"Wait here," he said, and he disappeared behind a door. He returned a minute later accompanied by a blond guy in his early twenties. The blond guy was pure muscle, too. "Peter Volz," he said, sticking out his hand. "I'll be your trainer."

I told him my name. "This is Drew," I said.

Peter led us to the main workout room. There were about two hundred machines, a whole section full of free weights, and only about twenty guys working out. My dad was right; there'd be no dead time. "Okay," Peter said. "Let's get to it."

He had us do hack squats, leg extensions, and bench

presses on a brand-new Smith machine. Peter was very particular about form; every time I did something, he'd put his hand on my arm or leg to show me what I was doing wrong. I tried to listen, but whenever he touched me all I could think was *Is this guy gay?* A couple of times I looked over at Drew and I knew he was thinking the same thing.

After what seemed like six hours but was only sixty minutes, Peter stopped. "Well, that's it," he said. "What do you think? You want to sign up for more sessions?"

Drew looked at me. I stood, frozen.

Peter Volz shrugged. "Hey, don't sweat it. You change your mind, I'll be here."

Once we were outside, we started laughing. "I am never going back there," I said.

"Me neither," Drew said. "Though the guy probably wasn't gay."

"I know," I said, "but the way he was always touching me was too weird."

. . .

When my dad came back from Miami, he asked how I'd liked Popeye's. "Not too much," I said.

"So you're not going back."

I could tell he was angry. "I lift at school," I said.

He shrugged. "It's up to you, Mick. But you've got the chance to use a state-of-the-art facility—"

"Mike," my mom said, "he doesn't want to go."

He threw his hands up. "Fine, Mick. Suit yourself."

10

A COUPLE OF WEEKS LATER I got into it with Nolan Brown, a junior tackle and one of Drager's friends. We were doing curls side by side in the school weight room. When Brown finished his set, he put down the barbell and turned on me. "You're one lucky son of a bitch, Johnson. You know that, don't you? Everything gets handed to you."

"What got handed to me?" I said.

He laughed. "What got handed to you? The starting spot on the team, that's what. If Matt were still around, your butt would be sitting on the bench next year."

I put the barbell down. "What makes you so sure I'm not better than Drager?"

Brown snorted. "What makes me so sure? Do you think that Foothill kid would have stopped Matt Drager, one-on-one, the way he stopped you? Do you think Matt would have come up one foot short?"

"No," I said, my face burning. "I think Drager would have come up two yards short."

It took Brown a second to figure out what I meant. When he did, he shook his head. "Very funny, Johnson. Ha, ha."

Once Brown moved off to another station, DeShawn came over. "Mick, every word you say to Brown goes right back to Drager. You know that, don't you?"

"I don't care."

"Yeah? Well, you should care. No sense in smacking a hornets' nest with a stick."

The next day I was eating lunch in the commons. I'd poured my milk into a glass and added the protein powder. I was starting to stir when Drew leaned toward me. "Don't turn around, but Drager and Clark are headed our way."

I kept stirring, but I could feel them reach our table, feel them stare over my shoulder. "What's that crap?" I looked back. It was Drager.

"It's a protein shake," I said.

"What do you take it for?"

"To get stronger."

"What do you need to get stronger for? I thought you were the strongest guy in the school. That's what you've been telling everybody, isn't it?"

I didn't answer. I put the spoon down and lifted the

glass to my mouth. Before I could drink it, Drager grabbed it out of my hand, took a sip, grimaced, and then spit it out over the rest of my food. I jumped to my feet and faced him, my hands balled into fists at my side.

He grinned. "Oh, sorry. Did I ruin your lunch? I didn't mean to; it's just that that stuff you drink tastes like crap and piss mixed together."

"What's going on there?" I looked past Drager and saw Mr. Chavez, the vice principal, hustling toward us.

Drager was up in my face. "Nothing's going on here, Mr. Z. We're just talking."

Chavez pushed himself between us. "Don't give me that, Drager. I'm not stupid."

Drager leaned back. "Ask him," he said, pointing to me.

Chavez turned to me. "Is there a problem here?"

"I'm fine," I said. "No problem."

Drager rapped the tabletop twice, then looked at Chavez. "See, Mr. Z. Nothing's happening. Just a friendly chat, that's all." He looked back to me. "We'll finish this another time, Johnson." Drager and Clark turned and walked away.

Mr. Chavez watched them go. "Drager gives you trouble, you tell me. You don't try to take him on. You understand?"

11

A COUPLE OF DAYS LATER, just after Coach Carlson had left the weight room to do his custodial work, Drager and Clark slipped inside. "Hey, you guys change your minds? You coming back?" Brad Middleton asked, a big smile on his face. That was Brad.

Matt Drager scowled. "No, Middleton, we're not coming back. I wouldn't play for Carlson if he got down on his knees and begged me."

"So what are you doing here?"

Drager nodded toward me. "I wanted to see just how strong Muscle Boy over there has gotten. Taking protein powders and lifting weights every day—I figure he must be a mountain man by now."

With that, Drager strode over to where Drew was doing bench presses. "How much weight you got on that barbell?"

"One twenty," Drew said.

Drager snorted. "One twenty. Put on a hundred eighty." Then he turned to me. "That's the weight NFL teams use to see how strong a guy is. Can you press it, or do you need to drink some barf powder first?"

"I can press it," I said.

"So let's see you do it."

With Drager and Clark and the rest of the guys watching, I slid onto the bench. Middleton eased the barbell into my hands. I got a good grip and pushed it straight up. Once . . . twice . . . three times. I could feel my face turning red, feel the veins on my forehead and neck filling with blood. My arms were wobbling, but I pushed it up a fourth time, a fifth. I might have made one more but Middleton snatched the weight away from me.

Drager clapped real slow as I stood, and then he stripped his shirt off. "My turn," he said, settling onto the bench. Again Middleton spotted him. Now the entire team was crowded around.

He was older than I was, and he was strong, but he hadn't been in the weight room once that winter. I expected he might match me or even beat me by a couple of reps, but he pumped one hundred eighty pounds the way I pumped one hundred twenty. He did five reps in about five seconds. He flew right through ten. He slowed a little at fifteen, but when he stopped at twenty, everyone knew he had more in him.

Middleton took the barbell from Drager, who stood and then wheeled on me, pointing his finger. "Still think you'd beat me out?" he said, coming toward me so that we stood nose to nose. "What's the matter, you little puke? Got nothing to say?"

I should have gone for his gut. If I'd hit him in the gut, he'd have lurched forward and I could have followed with a fist to his face and then maybe I'd have had him. But I went for his head because I wanted to hit him so hard he'd go down and stay down. He might have, too, had I connected.

But he ducked out of the way and my punch barely grazed his ear. A second later Clark grabbed me from behind, pinning my arms against my sides. Then Drager drove his fists into my stomach. The punches came fast and hard, like pistons. After what was probably ten seconds but felt like ten minutes, Clark released me. I slid to my knees, both arms covering my gut. Clark kicked me, and when I rolled to my side, Drager spit in my face. "See you around, Muscle Boy," he said, and the two of them walked out.

Once they'd left, DeShawn and Drew bent over me. "You all right?" Drew said, pulling me to my feet. I was almost standing when my knees buckled, but I didn't let myself fall back down. Once I was all the way up, I pushed Drew away. "I'm okay."

"You're not okay," DeShawn said, and he took my elbow.

I shook free. "I'm okay," I choked out. "Just leave me alone."

Somehow I made it into the bathroom, staggered to a stall, stepped in, and slid the steel bar into place, locking it. Then I went down on my knees, this time to throw up. I knew DeShawn and Drew were just outside the door. "Go away," I gasped between retches. "Go away."

They left, their footsteps echoing on the tile floor.

I could have stayed in that toilet stall for an hour, but they were waiting for me—DeShawn and Drew and the rest of them. I forced myself to stand; I forced myself out of the stall; I forced myself to wash up even though my ribs ached each time I raised my hands to my face.

When I returned to the weight room, the other guys stopped what they were doing and looked over, but nobody spoke. I walked to the corner where the dumbbells were, picked up the twelve-pounders, and made myself do some curls. That burned. Every couple of minutes I'd catch somebody looking over at me. Each time the guy would quickly look away. They were my teammates, and they'd stood there and let Drager and Clark beat me. Two against one, and no one had done a thing. After a while, the first guy left. Then another guy, and two more, and then I zipped up my duffel and headed for the door.

I wanted to get into my Jeep and drive off, but Drew hustled to catch up. "I'm sorry, Mick," he said. "I know I should have done something, but it happened so fast. I thought it was going to be a fair fight—you against Drager. What Clark did was gutless. But I didn't see it coming. Nobody did. And when it happened, I froze. And just when I was going to jump in, that's when Clark let you go. It happened too fast."

I looked up at the sky. The wind was pushing black clouds toward us, and that fit, because there was a black cloud over our friendship and words weren't going to make it go away.

"I'm not blaming you, Drew," I finally managed.

"But I'm blaming me."

"Well, don't."

We'd reached the Wrangler. "If anything like this ever happens again," Drew said, "I'll be ready. I won't stand and watch."

"Forget about it," I said. "That's the best thing." I started the Jeep up, managed a small wave, and drove home.

. . .

My ribs were so sore, I didn't return to school for two days. My gut was an ugly yellow-purple from the bruising, and I had trouble eating. I could have stayed home a third day, but by then my mother was suspicious. "A twenty-four-hour flu does not last seventy-two hours," she said. "If you don't feel well enough to go to school tomorrow, you're going to the doctor's."

As I started up the stairs leading to the main entrance of the school, I heard a voice call out: "Mick. Wait." I turned. It was Kaylee Sullivan.

I'd known Kaylee since middle school when we'd done a science project on landforms together—known her and liked her. She is tall, with brown hair and brown eyes. She is also an athlete: a sprinter and a volleyball player. All year I'd seen her around Shilshole High and said hello every time. And every time she smiled and said hello back, but we didn't have any classes together, so that was as far as it went.

"I heard about what Drager and Clark did to you," she said as we walked into the building. "They are just animals—two against one like that. Animals and cowards. That's what everybody says. They'd have no friends if they were still here. None at all."

"What do you mean, if they were still here?" I said.

She looked confused. "They're gone. Didn't you know? The day they beat you up—that was their last day. That's why they did it; they knew they could get away with it. But if you told Mr. Z., he'd get them suspended from West Seattle."

I shook my head. "I'm not telling anybody."

"I had a feeling you'd say that."

I looked at her. "Do you think that's wrong?"

"No. I guess not." She paused. "Well, I've got to go to math now. See you around."

. . .

Kaylee wasn't the only person who approached me that day. So did her friends Natalie Vick and Heather Lee. So did Russ Diver, a fat guy in my last-period class who I've known since first grade. And so did a kid with green spiky hair who I didn't know at all. It was as if every single person in the school had heard every detail. They were all trying to be nice; they were all saying that two against one wasn't fair. But I didn't want pity.

For the rest of the week, I went straight from one class to the next, keeping my head down in the hallways. I ate lunch by myself on the steps leading down to the tennis courts. And when the school day ended, I walked straight to the parking lot, hopped in my Jeep, and drove home—skipping weight training.

That weekend my dad had me turn over the soil in a spot behind the shed where my mother grew vegetables. The earth was wet from all the rain, and my arms ached from the work. As I shoveled dirt, my muscles burning, I kept picturing Drager, on his back, bench-pressing one eighty pounds like it was nothing. Then I saw myself, straining every muscle but only managing a fraction of what he'd done.

It would have been okay if Drager had been a little stronger than I was. That would have made sense, even—he was older and outweighed me by fifteen pounds. But Drager was a lot stronger. And I knew there were other running backs on other teams, guys born naturally strong like Drager but who also worked the weights every day. Drager didn't put in the work, so I could see myself catching up to him. It would take time, but I'd do it. But how could I catch up to guys who were just naturally stronger than I was and who didn't dog it?

Monday I went back to eating lunch with Drew and DeShawn, but nothing felt right. One of them would say something and I'd laugh too hard, and then I'd say something and they'd laugh too hard. After school I returned to the weight room. Guys nodded to me, said "Good to see you," but basically they left me alone. On Tuesday, Nolan Brown came over while I was doing squats. "What those guys did sucked, and Drager is no friend of mine," he said, and then he returned to his station.

That week I hit the wall. Bench press, squats, curls—you name it and I was stuck. I looked at the clipboard where I kept track of my personal bests and I saw that if anything, I was slipping back. In the hall the next day I asked Carlson what I should do. He shrugged. "Everybody hits a dead spot. Keep working and you'll get past it."

For the next weeks I worked and worked, but nothing changed. Around me the guys were laughing, having a good time. I pretended I was, too. I pretended that the whole thing with Drager was over. Over and forgotten. But I kept picturing Drager grinning at me, mocking me.

One Friday night, after my third straight miserable week in the weight room, I was up in my bedroom listening to music, my mind working like crazy. I had an alarm set to remind me to drink my final protein shake. It started beeping and I automatically got up, stepped into my bathroom, and reached for the protein powder.

Then I stopped. I looked at that stuff, and I hated it. I thought of the work I was doing to pay for it: the painting, the pruning, and the cleaning. I might as well go back to eating Snickers bars and drinking Coke, because if I wasn't getting stronger, then all the sacrifices made no sense. My dream of being a big-time football player—it was just that . . . a dream.

"Mick," my dad called up from the stairwell. "Do you know where the bucket is?"

"I think it's in the yard," I called down.

"See if you can find it. Your mom's looking for it."

I went downstairs, out the back door, and started across the yard toward the shed. A full moon was shining down. I didn't see the bucket, but in the middle of the lawn I spotted an old football. Without thinking, I picked it up and tucked it tight against my chest.

I took a couple of steps, as if I were playing, and somehow I wasn't in my backyard in the moonlight anymore. Instead, I was in a big-time game under the lights, and tacklers were fighting through blocks, trying to get at me. Everything was confused, cluttered, closed. I had no chance, none; I was going down. But then I made a quick move, and found some space, and then made a second move. A tackler dived for my ankles but missed. I cut back and saw it—an opening. I darted through the hole; a final tackler tried to grab me high, but I shrugged him off, and a split second later all was open in front of me, open and green and empty, and I was running down the field, running and running until I'd run out of space, run through the end zone. I raised the football above my head, then spiked it onto the lawn. It landed just short of the hedge, took a crazy football bounce, and disappeared under the shrubbery. I stood there, trying to remember why I was out in the yard in the first place. It took a while, but I finally remembered the bucket.

12

I WASN'T GIVING UP, but I couldn't keep doing the same things. I'd worked as hard as anybody in the weight room. Still I wasn't big enough or strong enough to go one-on-one with a linebacker in the red zone. To get bigger and stronger, I had to go back to Popeye's. Sunday, while my mom was at her new church, I asked my dad if he could still get me a membership. "I thought you hated Popeye's," he said.

"You were right about the weight room at school. I'm not making much progress. And I don't think our coach knows much about weight training. It's all three sets of ten and that sort of thing."

"Yeah, that's how the old guys did it. In fact, that's how I did it. I'll call Popeye's and get you an hour a week with that trainer. What's his name? Or do you want a different guy?"

"His name is Peter Volz, and he was fine. He knew what he was talking about. I got it in my head that he was gay."

My dad snorted. "Mick, gay guys are in every gym. Fact of life. You've got to take what people have to offer, whoever they are."

While I washed the Jeep, he called Popeye's. I was drying it when he came outside. "Tuesday," he said. "Three-thirty with Peter Volz. You're all set."

. . .

At school on Monday morning, I took the stairwell leading down into the basement. I knew Carlson's office was somewhere down there, but I had never been in the school basement before. I wandered around awhile before I saw him through an open doorway. He was seated in front of a computer, his head in his hands, deep in study. "Coach," I said.

He motioned to me with his hand. "Come on in. This will just take a minute more." I stepped into the little office and sat down on a blue plastic chair. "I can check every square foot of the school from here," he said as I sat. "Lights and heat and alarm systems."

"I thought your job was pretty simple," I said, and then I was embarrassed, afraid I'd insulted him. "I mean—"

"It's okay, Mick. You don't have to explain. But there is one thing you should always remember: Nothing in life is simple."

He went back to his computer. A minute or two later, he hit the Enter key and then turned to me. "So what can I do for you?"

I explained to him about Popeye's, how my dad could get me a free membership, and how I was going to start training there after school instead of with the team. "I wanted you to know that I'll still be lifting even though you won't see me."

"I don't check on my players, Mick. I told you that."

"I know," I said, "but—"

"But you thought I might check on players." He smiled. "That's okay. I am glad you told me, because I'd like you to reconsider."

"Why?"

"Because friendship counts for something, too. You work out with guys, you form a bond. Fourth quarter, tight game, everyone's tired—that bond matters. See what I mean?"

I squirmed in my chair. "I'm stuck, Coach. I've been stuck for weeks. You told me I'd get through it, but I haven't. I came up short last time. I don't want to come up short next time." He leaned back in his chair but didn't speak. "So, is it okay?" I said.

"Your decision, Mick. You do what you think is best."

. . .

When Carlson had mentioned friendship, I'd felt a sting. It had been a month since the run-in with Drager and Clark. Nobody had forgotten about it—not me, not Drew, not DeShawn. We acted like friends. We ate lunch together, and most days I gave one or both of them a ride home at the end of the day. But I didn't meet up with them between classes; and at lunch and during weight training, they talked more and more with each other and less and less with me.

I could never make up my mind how I felt about the way Drew and the rest of my teammates had acted. Sometimes I'd think about them watching while Drager and Clark beat me up, and I'd feel betrayed. But other times I'd picture the whole thing reversed, picture those two guys pounding on Drew or DeShawn, and I'd wonder what I would have done. There was something scary-crazy in Drager's eyes, something almost everybody in the school felt. Ten, maybe fifteen seconds—that's how long the whole thing took. I wanted to believe I'd have jumped in right away, but would I have been any quicker? I didn't know for sure.

When weight training ended on Monday, DeShawn went back to the library to use the computers. Drew and I walked out to the Jeep together. "I can't give you a ride home anymore," I said once I started it up.

"You losing the Jeep?" Drew asked.

"No, it's not that. I'm not going to do my weight training at school. I'm going back to Popeye's."

He flinched. "Popeye's? Why?"

"They've got great equipment, that's why."

"But it was so weird."

"It wasn't that weird."

A moment passed. "Is this because of Drager? Is that why—"

"It's got nothing to do with him," I insisted, and then I paused. "Look, you're a quarterback. Nobody expects you to go busting tackles and carrying guys into the end zone. Fourth and one, you're going to hand me the ball and you're going to count on me to get that yard. I've got to get stronger, Drew, and I've got to do it fast. Popeye's gives me the best chance." Neither of us spoke for the rest of the ride. I pulled up in front of his house. "You okay for a ride tomorrow?"

"Hey, what is it? A fifteen-minute walk home? I'm fine. Don't worry."

13

I WAS ONE HUNDRED PERCENT certain about Popeye's, but I was still nervous driving to Fremont on Tuesday afternoon, and I grew more nervous when I saw the mirrors with the guys standing in front. What would Peter Volz think when he saw me? I remembered how I'd acted that day—had he suspected what I'd been thinking?

There was no turning back, though. I pushed the door open and saw Peter sitting behind the main counter. "Hey, what's up, Mick?" he said, sticking out his hand.

I shook it. "Nothing much."

Peter nodded. "I talked to your dad. He said you're not happy with your weight program at school."

"I don't feel like I'm getting stronger."

"Well, you've come to the right place. You'll have to work, but I can help you make that work more effective."

I nodded toward the gym. "Should we get started?"

"We need to talk a little first. Ever had a mango smoothie?"

"No," I said.

"Jamba Juice is right next door. Let's go."

I wanted to buy my own, but he wouldn't let me. "You sit down," he said, and he went to the counter and ordered. A couple minutes later he stuck a tall cup in front of me. I took a sip. It was cold and sweet. "It's great," I said. "Thanks."

He reached into his back pocket and took out his wallet. "There are a couple of things we have to clear up if I'm going to be your trainer," he said. He thumbed through his photos. Finally he took one out and dropped it on the table. He was on a beach, and he had his arm around a beautiful black girl wearing a bikini. "First of all, that's my girlfriend, Tamika. She can tell you that I'm definitely not gay."

"I never thought you were—"

He put his hands up to stop me. "Yeah, you did, Mick. Look, you're a kid. It's a strange world. But from now on, if I move your arm up or down on a barbell or I show you how far to bend your knee, you can't freak out on me, because if you do, we won't get anywhere. Okay?"

He could have made me feel foolish—foolish and childish and stupid. But there'd been no mockery in his voice. I took a deep breath and exhaled, and when I looked back at him, he smiled. "Okay?" he repeated.

"Okay," I said.

"Good. That's settled. Now clue me in. What's the real reason you're back? And don't say you want to get stronger. Tell me what makes you tick, what's driving you. The more I know about your goals, the better."

I swallowed. "This is going to take time."

"That's why I got us the smoothies."

I thought what I was saying would bore him, but the more I talked, the harder he listened. It was like talking to an older brother. Better, really, because guys I knew who had older brothers mostly complained about how mean they were. I told Peter about my dad, how he'd been great in high school and college but had fallen apart during training camp in the NFL, and how he'd kept that from me, and how I'd found out only about a year and a half ago. I told him how my dad had taught me football from the day I was born, how it was the only game I'd ever played, and how now it was my turn, and I was right there, so close, but that I needed to get stronger. "I feel like if I can succeed, in a way I'll be doing it for both me and my dad. Lots of times he makes me mad, but he taught me the game. I don't want to let him down."

Peter stirred his smoothie for a while. "Look, Mick, if you work with me, your muscles are going to burn. They're going to be on fire and then I'm going to tell you to do another rep. And then, when you're done with that one, I'm going to want you to do two more. So if you're here just for your dad, you should go back to your school and work out with your team. Nobody puts up with the kind of pain I'm talking about for dear old Dad. So what I need to know is, are you here for you, too?"

"What do you mean?"

"I mean . . . do *you* want to be a football star?"

There was a challenge in his voice. "Yes," I said, loud and clear. "I want to be a football star."

His eyes brightened. "That's what I wanted to hear. You supply the willpower and I'll supply the knowledge. Together, we'll get you there."

We fell silent. I stirred my smoothie, sipped, and stirred again. When there were only a couple inches left, I remembered my supplements. I reached down into my duffel, took them out, and used the last inches of the smoothie to wash them down.

"Let me see those," Peter said.

I handed the vials to him. "Are they okay? I drink protein shakes, too."

"The protein shakes for sure are good. There's nothing wrong with this stuff either. Putting good things in your body is never a waste of money. Only . . ."

"Only what?"

"Nothing. Let's get going."

For the next hour, Peter worked me incredibly hard, just like he'd said he would. Bench presses, military presses, curls, rows, squats. He had me do sets in a way that was completely different from Carlson. I started by doing eight reps at a light weight, and I ended up doing only three reps, but he had me add weight for each new set so that the final three seemed a hundred times harder than the first eight. As I lifted, he took notes on everything I did.

My muscles burned in a way they'd never burned at Shilshole. He saw the pain in my face. "I got to warn you, this is a light workout. Eventually you'll lift to total failure. Then you'll know what pain is."

When the session was over, he walked outside with me. A light rain had begun falling. "That was great," I said, reaching out my hand.

"Got a minute?" he said.

"Sure."

He motioned to an overhang at the side of the building and we walked there. He scratched the back of his neck, frowned. "Look, Mick," he said, "you're going to find out from somebody in the gym, so you might as well find out from me. Those supplements you're taking? They might get you a little bigger, but just a little. If you're after serious gains, there's other stuff that

145

produces better results much faster, stuff that a lot of guys in the gym use."

"What other stuff?"

"You know what I'm talking about—gym candy. I started with Dianabol when I was your age. Basically they're all testosterone or testosterone derivatives."

I could feel the blood rush to my face. "You're talking about steroids, right? Those things mess you up. Every coach I've ever had has said that."

Peter shrugged. "People say that Adam and Eve came from outer space. Just because people say something doesn't make it true." He paused. "You've got testicles, right? Listen to the words. Testicles . . . testosterone. You take testosterone and you'll just be doubling up with something that's natural, something your body makes all the time."

I shook my head. "No. Not steroids. I'm not taking steroids."

Peter put up his hands. "Hey, that's fine, Mick. I only wanted you to know what's available. You can get plenty strong just by lifting."

I started to leave, but after a couple of steps, I turned back. "I can come tomorrow?"

"You're a member. You can come whenever you want. I've got other clients, but when I'm not busy with one of them I'll check in with you. Our next full hour together will be Saturday. By then I'll have a series of workouts set up for you—what I want you to do each and every day of the week."

14

THOSE DAYS I WAS INCREDIBLY BUSY. Shilshole High had gone to an online grading program, and my mom had a password that let her check every assignment with every teacher, so I couldn't let school slide. After school I drove to Popeye's and lifted, with Peter woofing at me if my form was a fraction off. In my free time, I was working jobs around the house to pay for the Jeep and the supplements.

Peter knew his stuff. My personal bests in the bench press, squats, and leg press started going up. And I could tell my body fat was going down; in the mirror I looked more muscular. But I wasn't lifting and eating right to look studly on the beach—it was all for football. Could I get the hard yards in the red zone? That would be the test.

In early May, spring football began. Carlson ran it differently from Downs. "I heard Coach Downs never started freshmen," he told us. "Well, that's not how it is with me. I play the best players, period. If you're a junior with three letters on your jacket, and you shave twice a day, and some smooth-faced freshman whips your ass in practice, then you're collecting splinters and he's playing. Understood?"

In a way, it was a bad joke. I knew the upperclassmen at my position, knew that none of them could challenge me. But there was an eighth-grader, Dave Kane, who was definitely a player. He had good size and he was fast. His long blond hair seemed to stream behind him when he ran. When I told Drew he worried me, Drew waved him off. "Pretty boy like that, he won't like getting hit by some two-hundred-fifty-pound lineman. I bet he switches to wide receiver by Friday."

Mr. Stimes was back as trainer, but Carlson had five new assistants, older black guys just like him. Linebackers worked with one coach; linemen with another; wide receivers with another. Carlson worked directly with me and Drew and the other backs. Under his eye my technique—especially my footwork—improved. We had some full-contact drills, but not many. Mainly it was helmet but no pads, which made me itch for a real scrimmage, and I wasn't the only one. "When are we going to play?" Felipe Perez called out after four straight days of drills.

"We'll play on our final Friday," Carlson said, "but that's it. I'm not getting anyone hurt for no reason."

When I told Peter about the scrimmage, he told me not to lift that Thursday. "Save your strength." It was good advice, but it was hard to stay home. Before Peter, weight training had always been drudgery; now I was addicted.

At last it was Friday—full-contact four-quarter scrimmage. Carlson put Drew and me on the Black team. When I looked around at the other guys with us, I saw nothing but first-stringers. Across from us, on the Red team, was the first-string defense.

It was exactly the test I wanted.

After the kickoff, Drew and I and the rest of the Black team trotted onto the field. On first down, I took the handoff and worked toward the sideline, stretching the defense, my eyes searching for a place to cut back. I found it, turned upfield, and took three or four strides before somebody hit me. I went down, but not before I'd smacked him back a couple yards. I'd gained seven.

I wanted the ball again, but Carlson had Drew throw over the middle to our tight end, Bo Jones. Drew's pass was right in his hands, but Jones dropped it. On third down Drew threw another pass, this one to DeShawn, running a post pattern down the middle of the field. DeShawn was open, but Drew's pass was about two yards too long. We had to punt, and the Red team's offense took the field. I trotted off, my mind working. One carry for seven yards—a good start. Only, why hadn't Carlson called my number on second or third down? Why the passes?

The Red offense was going up against the second-string defense, and those guys weren't as good. Dave Kane gained four yards on first down, two on second down, and then thirteen on a third-down draw play that caught the defense by surprise.

Three plays—and Carlson had called Kane's number three times. After a screen pass, Kane bulled his way for twelve yards straight up the middle. Drew had said he was soft, but he wasn't looking that way to me. Two downs later—on a third-and-three play—he took a short pass in the flat and with his speed turned it into a thirty-eight-yard touchdown. As Kane trotted off the field, Carlson was clapping his hands. "Way to run the ball! Way to run the ball!"

For the rest of that scrimmage, a calculator was running in my head, keeping track of both Kane's yards and my own. In the middle of the third quarter, he had me by thirty yards. Then, late in the fourth quarter, he took a handoff straight up the middle and bounced off the pile, and the next thing anyone knew he was racing down the sideline—sixty-five yards for a touchdown.

"One more series," Carlson shouted as Drew and I and the other first-stringers headed onto the field after the kickoff. "Let's kick some butt," I said in the huddle, "go out in glory." The guys nodded, but the fire was out. They were tired and wanted the scrimmage to end.

Carlson let Drew call all the plays on that drive, and Drew called my number. I gained eight yards on my first carry, a dozen more on the next one. "Keep giving me the ball," I pleaded, even though I was exhausted, and he did. Five yards, seven yards, four yards.

We drove down to the fourteen-yard line. On first down, I took a pitchout and broke for the corner. I made it and cut upfield, and there was the end zone in front of me. All I had to do was churn out those final yards and I'd have matched Kane—outplayed him, really, because I'd faced the first-team defense.

I never saw who hit me. All I know is that he got me from behind and that as he brought me down, he pounded his fist on the ball. It came loose and rolled slowly toward the end zone. I reached for it, but it was just beyond my fingertips. And then some cornerback scooped it up and started running. I twisted around to see Drew dive for him, but miss, near the twenty. Then I watched, helpless, as he took my fumble the length of the field for a touchdown. When he crossed the goal line, Carlson blew his whistle. "All right, men, that's it."

I dragged myself into the locker room and listened to Carlson tell us how we'd done okay but that we had to do better. "We can't practice as a team until August," he said. "I wish we could, but the rules are the rules. Until then, you guys keep in shape. Work out with one another. The field is yours in the morning, every morning, all summer long. And that weight room will be open every day for the rest of the school year, and Monday through Friday in the summer, too. That's it. Dismissed."

I started for the door, but before I reached it, Carlson called me back. "Mick, you ever play another position?"

"Not really," I said. "I've always been a running back. Why?"

"Just wondering."

I walked out, numb. It was part exhaustion, part failure, and part shame. Being beaten out by Drager had been terrible, but at least he was older than I was. But Kane? Kane was two years younger. And another position? I didn't know any other position. You've got to have passion to live through the pain of playing football. My dreams were a running back's dreams — cutting back, finding the hole, breaking into the open, running free.

I drove home and showered. My mom came in from work and fixed dinner. Afterward, I climbed upstairs to my room and sat on my bed, the lights off. I heard the phone ring, and then I heard my mom knock on my door. "Mick, it's your father. He's on commercial break."

I took the phone from her. "So? How'd the scrimmage go?" he asked.

"Fine. It went fine."

"Are you first team?"

"I don't know for sure."

"Come on, Mick. Are you first team?"

I paused. "I think I am."

His excitement came through the phone. "That's great. I'll warn Lion that I'll be taking off Friday nights next fall."

PART FOUR

1

SATURDAY MORNING, I was at Popeye's at nine sharp. "How'd the scrimmage go?" Peter asked as soon as he saw me.

"Could we talk?"

"Sure," he said. "Come into the back."

I followed him to the meeting room behind the main counter. The table had a bowl of bananas in the center. "Not so good?" he asked as he sat, taking a banana out of the bowl.

I sat across from him. "Tell me about that stuff again."

"What stuff?"

"You know."

"The Dianabol? What do you want to know?"

"You're sure it's safe?"

"I took it for a year. I do different things now, but I never had any problems."

"And I'd notice a difference?"

"Yeah, definitely. You'll be able to lift more, and you'll

be able to lift longer. People know steroids make you stronger. But stamina—that's where they help, big-time."

"Could I take them for a while, say until school starts, and then stop?"

He nodded. "Guys go off and on steroids all the time."

"Are you sure?" I said. "I don't want to get addicted to anything."

"Mick, it's like this. Once guys get going on the candy, they like the results. They keep taking steroids because they don't want to stop, not because they can't stop. But if someday you decide to quit, I promise you that you're not going to roll around on the ground crying and screaming like some wild-eyed heroin user desperate for a fix."

I took a deep breath and exhaled. "How much would it cost?"

"About the same as what you're spending on the stuff you're taking now."

"No more?"

"Maybe ten, twenty bucks a month more."

"Should I keep taking the stuff I'm taking now?"

"The protein shakes are good, but dump the pills."

"How soon could I start?"

"I've got product in my locker right now. You could

start today."

"Today?" I said. "You mean right now?"

"Why not?"

I took out my wallet and opened it up. "I've only got twenty dollars with me."

"That's okay. Twenty will get you going." He paused. "Do you want to do this, or not?"

I swallowed. "I want to do it," I said, and then I slid him the twenty dollars.

"Wait here," he said, and he left the room.

When he came back, he sat down next to me, opened a plastic vial, and shook out four white tablets that were about three times as thick as aspirin. "Guys just call it D-bol."

I looked at them, but I didn't pick them up. "So I take these and I get bigger?"

He shook his head. "Not that easy. You have to work out even more than before. But it's better, because the results are bang, right there."

"So do I just take them right now?"

"Slow down a second. There are things you need to know. You have to be careful about dosage and about how long you're on it—otherwise D-bol will do some gross things to you."

"Gross like what?"

Peter frowned. "Like you start growing breasts."

I felt my head jerk back as if I'd been slapped.

He put his hands up to reassure me. "I know it sounds creepy, but really, it's good. A side effect like that keeps you from abusing the stuff. As soon as you see it starting to happen, you stop taking the D-bol. I'll give you some pills that clean out the bad things. You'll lose some strength, but once your system is cleaned out, you go right back on the D-bol."

"And you have the other stuff, the stuff that keeps me from looking look like a girl?"

"It's called Nolvadex. And Mick, I would never give you the D-bol without having the Nolvadex ready for when you need it. Never."

I looked in his eyes, and I knew he was telling the truth. I picked up one of the pills and rolled it around in my fingertips. "How long before I'll see changes?"

"Four or five days. The first thing you'll notice is you'll be able to work out longer and lift more. There are other cool things, too. You got some sore muscle or pain in your back, you take these, and it'll be gone."

I thought how close I was. I wouldn't need much to win my job back from Dave Kane. "But for sure I'd be stronger by August?"

He nodded. "Mick, you do the D-bol and you keep

lifting weights and eating right—you do *all* those things and you will definitely be stronger by August." He paused. "So what do you say? You ready?"

I fingered the pills on the table. "I'm ready."

Peter went to the sink, poured me a glass of water, and slid it to me. "Your body puts out testosterone during the night, so you take D-bol in the morning. Start with four pills a day. Later you might go to six, but we'll see about that."

I put two of the pills in my mouth, took a big gulp of water, and swallowed them down. Then I picked up the other two and did the same. He handed me the plastic bottle and I slipped it into my duffel.

"Two more things," he said. "Being on steroids is like being on a roller coaster. Sometimes, you'll get a kind of screw-the-world feeling. You feel secretly strong and confident, like Tobey Maguire just before he transforms into Spider-Man. It's actually kind of cool so long as you don't let it blow up into full-force 'roid rage—and it won't if you don't let it."

"What's the other thing?" I asked.

"The other thing isn't cool at all. Sometimes steroids can turn the whole world into a black hole. I'm talking serious, dangerous depression. Watch out for that, too. I want this stuff to help you, Mick, not mess you up."

2

THE D-BOL KICKED IN Thursday. I was doing my usual sets of squats. I'd reached the last ones, the ones that always burned like a hot iron, and I breezed through them. I was able to do one more complete set before the fire came. I went over to the free weights and did some presses, and it was the same thing. After that I did calf raises and dead lifts and hit the cable machine for rows. I was looking around for something else to do when Peter came over. "It kicked in," I said softly. "I'm sure it did."

"Pretty awesome, isn't it? You're on the train now. You'll be surprised how fast it moves." He paused. "Go home, Mick. Eat. Sleep. When you come tomorrow I'll have a whole new workout schedule for you."

I drove home, rap music blasting. I was on such a high that I reached for my cell phone to call Drew and tell him before it hit me that I couldn't tell Drew or anyone on the team anything, ever.

. . .

The next day, I spotted Peter by one of the elliptical machines, showing an older guy how it worked. I was anxious to talk to him, but Peter stayed with the old guy for twenty minutes before he finally came over. "Let's go in the back," he said.

Once we were sitting down, he pulled out three typed pages and laid them down in front of me. "This is your program from now on."

The days of the week were written across the top of each page. Underneath were the focus muscle groups. And underneath that he'd listed the specific lifts I was to do along with the reps. Monday and Thursday were for my back and my legs. Tuesday and Friday it was my chest and my shoulders and my arms. Wednesday and Saturday he had me working everything.

I couldn't believe how detailed it all was and how many reps he expected me to do. "How come you didn't give me anything like this before?" I asked.

"You weren't taking D-bol before. You couldn't have done it."

3

I HAD NOTHING AGAINST Russ Diver. In fact, I've always liked the guy; everybody liked the guy. He was completely harmless, the class clown, the jolly fat guy. But as the final weeks of the school year wound down, I found myself disliking him. Whenever I saw him, a physical revulsion would come over me, a revulsion that seemed to grow and grow.

On the second to last day of school, I was walking down the hall when Diver came around the corner, laughing his big fat-guy laugh and not looking where he was going. He smacked right into me, knocking my backpack out of my hand and sending my stuff flying all over the place.

"Dumb me," he yelped, slapping himself on the forehead, an idiotic smile on his face.

He was reaching down to pick up my books. Instead of letting him do it, I lost it, like a volcano that erupts without warning. I grabbed Diver by the shoulder and pinned him against a locker. The smile was gone from his face; fear was written in his eyes. "Let me go, Mick," he said. "Let me go."

The whole time I held him, I knew I was acting crazy. I wanted to stop, but then Diver started crying, and that made me even more crazy-mad. I yanked him away from the locker and then slammed him back into it, the metal clanging from the force. That was when somebody grabbed me from behind. I spun around, fists clenched.

It was Drew. "Easy, Mick." His hand gripped my forearm. I tried to pull away, but Drew held tight. "Don't do anything stupid." His voice was quiet, but his eyes were intense.

For ten seconds he held my arm, and then I felt the anger subside.

"Get out of here, Russ," Drew said, looking over my shoulder. Instantly Diver disappeared down the hall. Drew looked around at the other kids who were still gawking. "The rest of you, get out of here, too." Slowly, they moved off, looking back over their shoulders at me. Finally Drew let go of my arm.

"What was that all about?"

"He knocked my stuff onto the ground," I said. "Besides, he annoys me." As I spoke I knew how stupid I was sounding.

Drew groaned. "Get real, Mick. Russ didn't mean anything. You hit him and you'll get suspended from school, which means a suspension from the team. You trying to give your position to Dave Kane? Besides, hitting Russ Diver? That's not you."

Drew crouched down and started gathering up my books. I watched for a while, knowing he was one hundred percent right, before I got down and helped him.

"Thanks," I said, once my junk was shoved in and the backpack was zipped shut.

"I owed you," Drew said. "I still do."

4

THAT WAS THE FIRST TIME the 'roid rage came over me, but once that edgy feeling came, it never entirely left. Most of the time it was no big deal—like having a tiny rock in my shoe that I couldn't get rid of. But every once in a while, it was as if I were a downed electrical wire after a huge storm. In those moments, if somebody nudged me, even a little, I could feel the bolts of electricity raging through me. I had to be very, very careful to keep myself from tumbling over the edge.

That was the bad thing about the D-bol; the good thing was simple—it worked. While I'd been on the supplements and the protein drink, I'd gained a pound every three or four weeks. With the D-bol, I was gaining nearly a pound a week, and I was setting personal bests almost every day.

I didn't mess around with the team's summer workouts. Instead, first thing in the morning I'd drive across the Ballard Bridge to Seattle Pacific University. I'd run on their rubberized track, three miles for endurance and then interval work for strength. After that I'd go to Popeye's, take my D-bols, and do my lifting. I could almost feel my muscles growing every day, my stamina increasing. Once you start getting bigger, you just want to keep getting bigger. Peter had said it felt like being on a train, but there were days when I felt like I *was* the train.

My workouts were so intense that by noon I'd have exhausted myself. I'd come home, eat lunch, and then start working on my dad's summer project—painting the house. I started with sanding and scraping the peeling paint. Everything took four times longer than I figured. Most days I worked five hours, but that was okay. The D-bol was expensive, so I needed to earn as much money as I could.

My mom would come home around six-thirty. She'd make me dinner, and then I'd go upstairs and play video games or watch TV. After about a week, she asked me where Drew was. "He's around," I said.

"How come I don't see him?"

I shrugged. "He hangs out with DeShawn mainly."

"I thought the three of you hung out together."

"Mom, I'm busy. I run, I do my lifting; Dad has me painting. I don't have time to hang out."

Her eyebrows knitted. "It's summer. You're sixteen. I want to see you having fun."

"I'm doing exactly what I want to do," I said. "Everything's fine."

That's what I said, but lots of nights I'd start playing Halo or some other video game and ten minutes later I'd turn it off. Then I'd lie back and wonder what Drew was doing. A couple of times I thought of calling him, but I knew he'd ask me how things were going at Popeye's. I didn't want to talk about that.

5

A LITTLE BEFORE SCHOOL had let out, I started getting the zits. For a while there were just a few, and I wasn't sure it was the D-bol causing them. But then more and more appeared, mainly on my back and chest. I kept a shirt on, always—even when it was hot—and after a while in the bathroom I used only the night-light so I wouldn't have to see them. I could have lived with the zits for a long time, but then something grosser happened. It was the first day of July, about six weeks after I'd started with the D-bol. I took a shower and as I dried myself off, I noticed that my nipples looked puffy and thick. Maybe I was imagining things, but the next day they looked worse.

I sucked up my courage and told Peter. "That's good," he said, putting his arm around my shoulder and walking me toward a corner of the gym. "Your telling me right away, I mean. I've known guys who hide it, hoping it will go away on its own. It doesn't."

"So what do I do?"

"Wait here," he said.

A couple of minutes later he came back with a small brown bag. Inside was a vial of pills.

"I told you I'd never leave you hanging, didn't I? You stop taking the D-bol and you take these instead. They'll clean you out."

"For how long?"

"Hard to say. Two weeks, maybe less. Everybody's different. Once your body gets back to normal, you can take the D-bol again."

"But if I don't take D-bol for two weeks, won't I slip back?"

He looked at me sideways. "Yeah, you will. I told you that up front. That's how D-bol is. Two steps forward, one step back."

"I can't step back now," I said, suddenly feeling desperate. "Football tryouts are in August. I've got to keep going forward."

"You've got no choice, Mick. Your body is screaming *Stop*."

I stared at him—he was rock solid. "How come you

don't have zits? How come you never lose muscle?"

"I've got zits," he said. "Not on my face, but on my back and chest."

"But you don't ever cut back on your workouts, do you?"

He bobbed his head this way and that. "No. Not really."

"So how come you can keep going and I can't?"

He shrugged. "I take different stuff from you."

"What stuff?"

"I take a combination of drugs. It's called doing a stack."

"Why can't I do a stack?"

"Because you wouldn't want to use the things I'm using."

"Why not?"

"Because you've got to inject yourself."

I stared at him. "You mean with a needle, like heroin?"

"With a needle, but not like heroin."

"You shoot up?"

"I give myself injections, but I don't do it to get high, and I'm not addicted to anything, so I wouldn't call it shooting up."

I nodded toward the gym. "The serious bodybuilders, do they shoot up, too?"

"Some do, some don't."

I shook my head back and forth. "I'm not sticking a needle in my arm. No way."

Peter threw his arms out. "Nobody's asking you to do injections. I knew you wouldn't want to, which is why I never brought it up. But just for you to know, you don't stick a needle in your arm—you stick it in your butt."

"I don't care where you stick it. I'm not doing it."

"I hear you, Mick. I hear you loud and clear. No injections." He took a deep breath. "Look. I've got other people I've got to work with. Take some time off. Get away from the gym. Don't come back until your system is cleaned out. Then we'll get you going on the D-bol again and you won't feel so bad about all this."

6

ONCE I LEFT POPEYE'S, I walked along the Fremont Cut. It was a hot day; sailboats were moving through the cut toward Puget Sound. I sat down on a bench by the bridge and looked out.

My mind was going a million times faster than the traffic on the bridge. I could feel the rage coming—only this time it wasn't directed at Russ Diver or anybody else. My rage was aimed squarely at me. The zits, the puffy nipples—they were betraying me. I hated my body, hated what it was doing. When I needed it to be strong, it had gone weak. *Two steps forward, one step back.* That sounds okay until the day comes when it's time to step back, and you find out it isn't okay.

Bells started clanging and the Fremont drawbridge slowly rose, allowing sailboats through. Traffic backed up; gulls wheeled in the sky. A huge sailboat glided past. The bridge slowly came down again. I walked back to the Jeep and drove home.

At home, my dad took me into the yard and showed me how to work a power washer he'd rented. I climbed a ladder and washed the second story, water spraying everywhere, drenching me. After lunch I cleaned the ground floor, finishing at two-thirty. I would have to let the siding dry for four days before I could paint. The whole day—the whole week—stretched out in front of me. And it was right then, almost as if by a miracle, that my cell phone rang.

"Hey, Mick," Drew said. "What's up?"

"Nothing," I said, glad to hear his voice.

"Really?" he said in disbelief. "You really got nothing going? I thought you had every minute of the summer planned out. Workouts at your gym and work for your dad and all that."

"I'm taking a short break from my workouts. I just power-washed the house, and it's got to dry out before I can paint. So I've got nothing going."

"Well, that's great," he said, his voice excited, "because I was hoping you'd want to hang out some but I didn't figure you'd have time."

"I've got time."

"All right, then, here's the deal. DeShawn and I have been going to Green Lake in the afternoons to play volleyball with Natalie, Heather, and Kaylee—that group. Brad Middleton has been coming, but he just left for Scotland with his family. We need another player." He paused. "It'll be fun, and Kaylee especially will like seeing you. She's got a thing for you, I think. What do you say?"

"When's all this happening?" I asked.

"Now," he said. "Well, not right now, but in half an hour. The big field across from Starbucks."

I felt like a drowning man in the ocean who suddenly sees a boat heading his way. "I'll be there. I can give you a ride if you want."

"Thanks, but I don't need one. I got my permit last week. My dad will drive down with me. He wants me to get practice on hills."

. . .

173

First I had trouble finding a parking spot near the lake, and then, as I walked toward the lake, a feeling of panic came over me. I hadn't hung out with anyone for a long time. I wasn't sure I knew what to say or how to act. I considered turning around and going home, but Kaylee saw me and waved. She was wearing light blue shorts and a white tank top. Her hair was pulled back in a ponytail, and her whole body was tan and somehow seemed to glow.

Heather and Natalie were there, too, along with Drew and DeShawn. I joined in the large circle and tried to warm up with them. I felt useless until Kaylee took me to the side and showed me how to bump a volleyball. Sometimes I was decent, but about every third hit would go careening off wildly. I felt certain I'd ruin the game for everyone, but Kaylee only laughed. "You'll get it, Mick. It takes time."

Nets were set up for pickup games all around the field. The rules were simple. Win and you keep playing; lose and you sit out. DeShawn and Kaylee were great, the other girls were good, Drew was okay, and I was up and down, occasionally making decent shots but at other times fouling up easy balls. We lost more than we won, but nobody seemed to care.

Around five we went over to Guayma's and ate

nachos, and then we walked around Green Lake, paired up. "See you tomorrow?" Kaylee said when we were back at the field.

"Yeah," I said. "See you tomorrow."

7

FOR THE REST of the week, I spent every afternoon playing volleyball and then walking around Green Lake afterward with Kaylee. Every time I looked at her, she seemed brighter and more alive. Sometimes talking to her was awkward, but other times we'd get going and the words came naturally. On Thursday and Friday, I drove Kaylee home. "It's cool that you have your license," she said.

"I didn't get held back or anything," I said. "My dad just didn't start me when I was five."

"My parents did the same thing with my younger brother," she said.

Saturday the plan was to play volleyball, walk the lake, eat at the Green Lake Café, and then see a movie at the Majestic Bay. When I left the house after lunch, I told my mom I'd be home late. "Good," she said. "Glad to hear it."

Parking was much harder than usual by Green Lake. As I neared the field, I could tell something was different. Instead of pickup volleyball games, a tournament was going on. Around the outside of the field were booths selling volleyballs, visors, kneepads, and ankle braces—all that stuff.

It was a hot day, the hottest day of the summer. I spotted Kaylee and the others under a tree in a circle, bumping the volleyball. The girls were wearing shorts and bikini tops. Kaylee's was white, and it made her tan more golden.

I joined the circle. "Can we play in the tournament?" I asked.

"We can play," Drew answered, "but it costs fifty bucks to enter."

"Fifty bucks," I asked.

"Fifty bucks," he repeated. "And when we lose twice, we're out."

We bumped a little longer, until finally Natalie Vick caught the ball. "We've got to decide."

"I say no," said DeShawn. "We got no chance. It's a waste of money."

"So what are we going to do instead?" Kaylee said.

"How about we go swimming?" Drew suggested. "We could swim and then walk around the lake to dry off."

Within minutes the girls were in the water, with

Drew right behind them. DeShawn had been wearing high-top basketball shoes, so it took him time to unlace them. "I'll stay up here and watch everybody's stuff," I said to him.

"Nobody's going to take anything," he said.

"I don't feel like swimming."

DeShawn shook his head. "It's a zillion degrees, there are three girls out there in little bikinis waiting for you, and you don't feel like swimming? You're nuts."

He turned, ran down the beach, and dived into the water. I saw Kaylee talking to him, and then she swam toward me. "Come in the water, Mick," she called out. "It's not cold. Really." Then Heather and Natalie started calling for me to join them.

I didn't know what to do. I'd been taking the Nolvadex for nearly a week. I thought my nipples had pretty much gone back to normal, but I still had some zits on my back and chest.

The girls kept waving and calling. Other people on the beach were starting to stare. I felt like an idiot, so I took off my shoes and shirt and raced into the water until it was knee high, then dived and swam out to them. I stayed hunched down, treading water, only my head visible. The girls were doing the same thing, hiding their bodies.

We splashed each other for a while, and then

DeShawn and Drew swam over to a pier that juts into the water, climbed up, and dived off. Soon Heather and Natalie started diving, too. "You want to dive?" Kaylee asked.

"Not really," I said.

After about ten minutes, the rest of them climbed out and sat on the pier in the sun, talking and sunbathing. "You want to sit on the pier?" Kaylee asked.

"You go ahead. I'll just go back to the beach and dry off."

"I'll get out, too," she said.

"No, don't," I said. "Stay with them."

"Only if you do."

What could I do? I liked her; I didn't want her to think I was weird. Besides, I wasn't really sure if anybody would notice anything. It's not as if I were the only high school guy in the world with a few zits on his chest and back. So I swam over to the pier, grabbed hold of the ladder, and pulled myself up. Kaylee had climbed up before me and was just sitting down. As soon as I stepped onto the wood planks, she looked at me. She'd been smiling, and then her face dropped.

I looked down at my body. In my bathroom with a night-light on, my chest hadn't seemed too bad. But out in the bright sunlight, there was no pretending. My nipples were still oddly puffy, and my zits were red and angry.

Kaylee had caught herself. The revulsion was gone from her face; in its place was a phony cheerfulness. The rest of them were the same. When they looked at me, they made sure that they looked only from the neck up.

I forced myself to sit there, for a minute . . . for two minutes . . . for three. Then I stood. "I've got to go now," I said. "My dad needs me to help him paint." Before anyone could object, I walked the length of the pier, back to the beach.

I dried myself a little with my shirt and then pulled it on. How stupid could one person be? I looked back for a split second. Kaylee had stayed on the pier with the rest of them, which was where I wanted her to be.

Once I got into my Jeep, I turned the radio on full blast and drove, taking every turn hard and fast. I drove east on Forty-fifth, away from Green Lake, from my home, from Shilshole High, from Popeye's, from everything. I was headed nowhere, just away. I wasn't sure if I wanted to think or if I wanted to keep myself from thinking.

I followed Forty-fifth out to I-5 and headed south. When I saw the turnoff for I-90 a couple miles later, I took it and then drove up into the mountains toward eastern Washington, where I used to go camping with my dad. As I drove, my mind was racing. What did I want, really?

In Ellensburg I bought a sandwich in a supermarket and ate at a picnic table at a rest stop. Then I got back in the car and drove another hour. Just outside Yakima I filled the tank at an Arco station. After I paid, I headed back to the freeway. I could have kept driving, through Yakima and south into Oregon, but what was the point? I was tired of thinking, tired of driving, tired of everything. When I exited the gas station, I took the Seattle on-ramp.

Instead of being crowded with a million thoughts, my mind shut down on the ride home. The setting sun turned the brown hillsides outside Yakima to gold. By the time I reached the mountains, it was deep twilight, the trees like shadows of themselves. I cleared Snoqualmie Pass a little past ten and reached the house around eleven.

8

Sᴜɴᴅᴀʏ ᴍᴏʀɴɪɴɢ, my mom pleaded with my dad and me to go with her to her new church, Mars Hill. "It's different from a regular church. Vibrant, intellectual, socially committed. The people are there because they want to be there. Just once, please. Spirituality is a part of life, too."

The service lasted from eleven to noon. The sermon was about making the world better in little ways. Afterward, cookies and coffee and Coke were served in the basement. My mom, her cheeks red, a circle of friends surrounding her, seemed like a different person. I'd never heard her talk so much or so fast. My dad got a cup of coffee and found himself a corner. I felt lost, and then over by the food table I spotted Russ Diver. Our eyes locked for a moment before he looked away, pretending he hadn't seen me.

Maybe it was listening to the sermon about doing the little things right. Or maybe it was that I didn't want to play the coward. Whatever the reason, I made myself walk over to him. "Hey, Russ."

"Hey, Mick," he answered, distrust in his eyes.

"You come here much?" I asked, trying to sound casual.

"Every week."

"This is my first time."

"Yeah, I figured." We stood, awkward and silent, and then he nodded toward an overweight girl who played clarinet in the school band and whose name I'd heard but forgotten. She was holding up a paper cup and smiling at him. "I've got to go, Mick," he said. "Gina's waiting for me." He started off toward her.

"Russ," I called, and he turned back. "I'm sorry about that day."

His eyes went wide. "I should have been looking where—"

"No, Russ," I said. "It was my fault."

He nodded before quickly turning and heading off.

For the next half-hour, I stood in a corner, feeling completely out of place. Every once in a while I'd look over at Russ and he'd be laughing with Gina, or she'd be looking up at him as if he were a prince and he'd be looking at her as though she were a princess. He was the fat, blubbery loser. I was the guy on the football team. How could he have everything squared away while everything was in pieces for me?

When I got home a message from Drew was on the machine. He rattled on and on, trying to act as if nothing had happened, but I could feel the tension in his voice. "Give me a call," he said at the end, "or just show up at Green Lake."

I listened to his message three times. It was another hot day, close to ninety. They'd want to go swimming at Green Lake, all of them, but if I was there, we could be ten feet from a lake and no one would even suggest it. They'd think they were being kind, but the silence would be humiliating. And it wouldn't just be today, it'd be all summer.

Maybe there was a way, though. Little by little, the Nolvadex was working. If I got off the train entirely, if I never took the D-bol again, then the grossness would never come back. I could swim, I could sunbathe, I could walk the lake with my shirt off. Whatever any of them wanted to do would be okay, because I wouldn't be disgusting.

I went downstairs, got into the Jeep, and headed out, not sure where. Driving along Fremont Avenue, I could feel the pull of Green Lake. Kaylee and Drew and Natalie and Heather and DeShawn—they were hanging out, talking, waiting for me. I thought again of Russ Diver and Gina. Okay, he was fat, and okay, she was nothing to look at—but still, they were happy being with each other, happy being themselves. I'd seen it in her eyes, in his. It could be that way for Kaylee and me.

All I had to do was turn left, circle around to Stone Way, and drive to the lake.

Maybe that's why I didn't do it. Because it was so simple. I could *always* make that turn and go to Green Lake. I could always stop the steroids, stop the workouts with Peter, stop going to Popeye's. I could always give up on my dream of being something special on the football field. I could always be another guy on the football team. Third row back, third from the end in the team photo.

I could always be a nobody.

9

PETER SPOTTED ME as soon as I stepped through the door. "Hey, Mick," he said. "Good to see you again."

"Good to be here," I said.

He lowered his voice. "How's your body doing? The stuff working?"

"Yeah, but slowly."

"You might always have some zits and some nipple puffiness. It varies from person to person."

For a moment we both stood, neither of us speaking. Then I said it. "I want to do a real stack."

He looked around the room. A couple of guys were within earshot. "Let's go in the back."

I followed him to the meeting room. "You're sure?" he said once the door clicked shut behind us.

"I'm sure."

"Why the change?"

"Because tryouts are coming up. I've got to be ready. The stuff you do—it'll make me stronger faster, right?"

"Yeah, it will." He lowered his voice. "But you're talking injections, you know, and a lot of them."

"I know."

"And you're okay with that?"

"I don't really know if I'm okay with it or not. I'll know after I try it. I don't have to keep doing it once I start, right? I mean, I can always quit."

"Sure, you can quit. It's not addicting."

"And it won't mess me up?"

"Not in three months it won't. Or even in three years. Thirty years of use—that's another story."

"I'm not worried about thirty years from now."

He nodded. "Neither am I." He paused. "Mick, there's one last thing to get settled—money. Doing a stack is going to cost you fifteen dollars a day. Can you cover that?"

I did the calculations in my head, combining how

much I'd saved with how much I could still earn. Tryouts were six weeks off. "Yeah, I can."

Peter nodded toward the main exercise room. "You go out and do some lifts while I line things up. In an hour or so, I'll have a kit ready for you."

I returned to the main training room and worked the dumbbells, keeping my eyes on the door to the back room, waiting for Peter to appear. At last the door opened and he motioned for me to rejoin him.

"Here's how it works," he said, once we were alone.

For the next few minutes he talked about testosterone and Deca-something and D-bol and Nolvadex. I was supposed to take these two pills for the first weeks and then that one for the next couple of weeks and give myself injections on Sunday, Tuesday, Thursday, and Friday. After that . . .

My head was spinning. Peter stopped. "Look, I'll get a calendar and write down what you should do week by week until your tryouts start. For right now, let's just get the hard part over with."

"The hard part?"

"Mick, you know what I'm talking about."

"You mean I'm going to do an injection right now?"

"Right now." He eyed me. "You can still change your mind."

I took a deep breath. "No, I'm ready."

"Okay, here's how it works. In the beginning, we'll be partners. You'll give me an injection, and then I'll give you one. After three or four times, you'll be on your own."

My mouth was so dry, I couldn't speak, but I did manage to nod.

He picked up a vial and held it in front of him. "Here's the most important thing: Think *clean.*" He dipped a cotton swab in isopropyl alcohol, pulled his shorts down a little, and spread the alcohol over the top part of his butt. Then he cleaned the top of the vial.

"Once you've got everything clean, take the needle out of the wrapper, insert it into the syringe, and draw it full of air like this." I watched as he pulled the handle all the way back. "Next, stick the needle into the vial and push the air in. See?"

I nodded.

"After you've done that, turn the needle and vial upside down and pull back on the needle to fill the syringe, like this. You're going to be taking two hundred milligrams each time," he said, "so go to about two twenty-five milligrams to compensate for any air bubbles. Once you've got the right amount, pull the needle out of the vial and then tap the plastic part of the syringe to get all the little bubbles out." I watched as he tapped it. "See how all the air moves toward the pin? Once that happens, push down on the syringe like this to force the air out of the needle. Don't stop until a few drops of the stuff run down the pin."

He handed the syringe to me. My hands were shaking so badly, I didn't think I could hold it. "Just relax, Mick. We're about ready." He pulled his shorts down a little again and reswabbed the injection site. "Clean," he said. "Always clean. You ready?"

"I guess."

"Okay. You're going to stick the needle in like it's a dart. Go ahead." I swallowed, then stuck the needle into his butt. "All right," he said. "That's good. Now slowly push down on the syringe." I pushed, just as I'd seen nurses push. It was way easier than I'd expected. "That's right," Peter said. "Just like that."

After about ten seconds, the syringe was empty. I removed the needle and threw it into the trash. Immediately, Peter dipped another cotton swab into alcohol, cleaned the injection site, and massaged the area. "Rubbing cuts down on soreness," he said. "Now I'll do you."

It seemed like it had taken me an hour to give Peter his stuff; it took about thirty seconds for him to inject me. "That wasn't bad, was it?" he said when he finished.

He put the stuff into a small travel kit and handed it to me. "Four times a week with this, Mick, and the four tablets every morning, and you're on your way. If the D-bol was like hitching a ride on an express train, this is like blasting off on a rocket. I'm talking an explosion." He raised a finger. "Just remember to watch out for the rage and even more for the depression. Guys have had spells of depression six months after they've stopped doing injections. Don't get too wound up, because when you unwind, you'll spin that much faster. If depression does come, you've got to fight through it."

I didn't go home. Instead I got out on the road and drove. You do something huge like injecting steroids, and you expect to feel hugely different. But I didn't. In fact, I had to keep telling myself over and over that I'd just done an injection, that I'd just started on a real stack. I took the ramp to Aurora Avenue and drove along the viaduct toward West Seattle. I had a CD playing, but I wasn't listening. In my mind, I was back in the Foothill game, only now I was stronger, now it was number 50 who had the turf give way, now he was crumpling and I was in the end zone. Was that really what the needle would do? Would it change everything?

When I got home, my mom told me Drew had called. When he had called me before, it had been as if I'd been thrown a life ring. Now, with one injection, every-thing had flipped one hundred eighty degrees. The zits would be coming back, but it wasn't just the zits I was hiding—it was everything.

I punched in his number.

"We missed you today at Green Lake," he said. "Kaylee especially. You coming tomorrow?"

"I can't, Drew. My dad is after me to finish painting the house before football starts. My afternoons are jammed."

"How long is it going to take?"

"I don't know. Maybe all summer."

"To paint your house?"

"He wants it done right. And starting tomorrow I'm going back to Popeye's to work out." I paused. "I can't let that Kane kid beat me out."

I could hear Drew sigh through the phone line. "Mick, we need six to play. If you stop coming, Natalie's going to ask Brad Middleton. When he comes back from Scotland. You hear what I'm saying?"

"There's nothing I can do. I wish I could play, but I can't."

"Okay," he said. "I wanted to make sure you knew the score."

When I hung up, I stared at the phone. It wasn't that

big a deal, I told myself. Sure, I wanted to hang out with Drew, with Kaylee, but you can't have everything. Six weeks—that was all I was giving up. After six weeks, football would start and I'd have two practices every day until the season started. Then there wouldn't be time to play volleyball, to walk the lake with Kaylee. In those six weeks I was giving up, I could transform myself. I could make myself into the player I wanted to be—and the payoff would be this season and the next season and the season after that.

. . .

Peter had said it would be like a rocket ride, but day in and day out it was just hard work. He had me double the time I spent lifting, and he had me work to total failure, where I actually had to drop the weights because I couldn't move them either up or down. I'd work out, drink some Gatorade, work out, work out, work out, work out. And when I finished at the gym, I'd run three miles at the Seattle Pacific track to keep up my stamina.

On Saturdays, Peter would take me to the back room and lay out which pills I should take when, the days I should do the injections, and the progress he expected from me. That first week, I did the injections with

Peter, but after that, I injected myself. Once an injection was done, a sense of power would rush through every cell of my body, and every time I looked at myself in the mirror after I showered, I seemed not only stronger, but also older—more like a man.

10

THE DEPRESSION HIT ME the day before tryouts. It came out of nowhere—it was as if I'd stepped into an elevator and the doors had closed and the elevator had started falling and falling, and there was no stopping it. Everything seemed pointless—the morning workouts, the weightlifting, the running, the steroids. Pointless. Pointless. Pointless. None of it was going to matter. I was certain I was going to fail. I was ugly and gross and I'd given up Kaylee, I'd shut the door on Drew, and it was all for nothing. I'd always fail, all my life, in everything. That's who I was.

Peter had told me exactly what to do when the blackness hits. "Move around," he said. "Do something, anything. The one thing you don't want to do is nothing, because if you do nothing, it will get worse."

His advice had sounded easy to follow. No big deal.

If depression ever hits me, I had thought, *I'll just play some video games. How hard can that be?* But now playing a video game seemed like the stupidest thing in the world.

My father saved me. Since it was Sunday afternoon, he was around. He tapped on my door, opened it a foot, and leaned in. "You doing anything?"

"Not really."

"Your tryouts are tomorrow, right? How about we toss the ball around a little?"

"I don't really feel like it."

"Come on. Do it for me. Whenever your season starts, I get the taste for it."

I had to force myself downstairs. Lacing up my shoes was a huge effort. But once I was outside, once I broke a sweat, the elevator stopped falling, reversed, and slowly came back up. By the time we finished, it was almost as if the depression had never happened.

Almost.

• • •

Monday morning, I felt strong. I took the D-bol first thing but waited until just before I left for practice to inject testosterone. On the way out, I pulled on the sleeveless T-shirt I usually wore. I looked at my arms.

They were muscular, defined. Would one of the coaches notice? Would they know? I took the shirt off and put on a baggy sweatshirt instead.

Carlson ran a crisp practice, much more focused than Downs's. They both ran the same drills—running through tires, hitting the sleds—regular football practice stuff. But there was no slack time with Carlson, while there'd been tons with Downs. The afternoon session was lighter, with more walk-throughs, more explanations, but he still moved it along.

Tuesday, practice turned serious. Carlson's assistant coaches were all over the field, clipboards in hand, timing this and that, seeing how far and how high we could jump, how strong we were.

An hour into Tuesday's afternoon practice, Coach Brower, one of the assistant coaches, called Middleton and me over. "I need to get a forty-yard dash time for both of you," he said in his gravelly voice.

Shilshole has a crushed-rock track—not exactly high tech. I'd always run 4.7 or 4.8 in the forty, not great, but not terrible considering the quality of the track. I knew I'd been running faster than that on the rubberized track at Seattle Pacific. Brower pointed to the start; I settled into position and waited, muscles tense.

"Ready . . . Go!"

I exploded forward, my arms and legs churning, my lungs filling with air. I was still picking up speed when I crossed the finish line. I slowed, then stopped and headed back toward Brower. Middleton came over to me. "Man, you were flying."

"I've got you in four fifty-two," Brower said to me, staring at his stopwatch. "That's two seconds faster than last spring. Middleton, you came in at five twenty-three." Brower looked up. "Run it again for me, okay?"

I ran my second forty in 4.51, despite a tiny slip at the start. After Brower wrote the number down, he eyed me closely. "How much do you weigh, Mick?"

"Almost two hundred," I said.

He whistled softly. "Two hundred, with that kind of speed. You are going to be a load to bring down."

We had two practices every day: pads and helmet in the morning, helmet only in the afternoon. Lots of it was conditioning and agility stuff—drop step and go left, drop step and go right, backpedal, explode. In drill after drill, I was at the top of the charts. "Come ready to play tomorrow," Carlson said on the second Wednesday. "Time to find out where we are."

11

THERE'S SOMETHING INCREDIBLE about pulling a helmet on just before a game; it's a feeling only a football player knows. Your vision narrows, and the whole world shrinks. You can't hear much of what goes on outside you, but you can hear yourself breathe and you can feel yourself sweat.

Drew and I were on the Black team again. The first play from scrimmage was a toss sweep for me. I took the ball on the dead run, looked up, and saw a freshman linebacker coming up on me.

The kid had taken the perfect angle. I couldn't juke him without going out of bounds, and I couldn't cut back without taking myself into the range of more tacklers. The only thing I could do was lower my shoulder to try to drive through him . . . so that's what I did.

I hit him, and he went flying like a bowling pin, his helmet rattling off as he smacked the ground. I saw the helmet rolling ahead of me, bounding crazily, but I kept my legs churning, gaining yards. Fifteen yards later, somebody pushed me out of bounds. When I turned to head back to the huddle, I saw the freshman. He was down on the ground, flat, looking as though he'd been shot.

Our trainer, Mr. Stimes, raced onto the field, with Carlson right behind him. Stimes cracked open some smelling salts and stuck them under the kid's nose, and he came to. His arms moved, and then his legs moved, and I could breathe again and so could everybody else.

You never want to hurt anybody, but once I knew he wasn't paralyzed, inside I was electric. I was a rocket. *That's what I can do now,* I thought to myself. Carlson looked over at me. It had been a hard hit, but it had been a clean hit. "Way to drive your legs, Mick."

The next two plays were passes, and then Drew called my number for a draw up the middle. The hand-off was a little sloppy, so I wasn't going full speed when I hit the hole, but I kept churning my legs forward, driving, driving. I don't how many yards I got, but I know it was at least ten.

Carlson had Drew stretch the defense by going deep to DeShawn. The play almost clicked, but the ball slid off DeShawn's fingertips. The next play was a screen pass to me. I blocked my guy for a two count and then slipped into an open area in the right flat. Drew's pass was on target. I watched it into my hands and only then turned upfield.

I got two good blocks and cut back toward the middle, and suddenly only the free safety was between the end zone and me. I bore down on him, but instead of holding his ground, he stepped to the side and waved at me as if I were a bull and he were a matador with a red cape. I broke right through his arm tackle, and then I was off, running straight into the end zone. Touchdown!

The guys on the Black team circled around me, screaming, but I kept a stone face. *When you get into the end zone, act like you've been there before and you're planning on being there again.* Those were Carlson's instructions, so that's what I did. I high-fived a couple of players, trotted to the sidelines, pulled my helmet off, and took a swig of water. Carlson glanced over his shoulder. "Nice running, Mick."

The Red team took over on offense, with Dave Kane in at tailback. By the time they ran their third play, Drew had planted himself next to me on the bench. "You were awesome," he said.

He kept talking and I managed to answer, but my eyes were on the field, watching Kane. I tried to see him the way Carlson was seeing him. Did he run hard? Did he run north-south? Did he block? Was he as good as I was? The answers came pretty quickly. Yeah, he ran hard. Most of the time he ran north-south. Yeah, he blocked. No, he wasn't as good as I was.

The Red team made a couple of first downs and then

punted. I pulled my helmet on, my world got small again, and I headed back onto the field.

All through that scrimmage, I was in the zone. When I needed a burst, I could feel my muscles explode. I was fast to the hole; I was strong through contact. I had more endurance than ever before. I felt as if I could play and play and never get tired.

When Carlson finally blew the whistle, he still had questions to answer about the team. Who was going to be our strong safety? Our right cornerback? Our kick returner? But there was no question about the featured running back, because that job was mine.

After practice, I was too pumped up to go home. I climbed into the Jeep, stuck an old Rolling Stones CD into the player, and pounded on the steering wheel as I drove out on Greenwood toward Shoreline. The wind was blowing in from all directions, and my hair was flying like my spirits.

I'd done it.

I'd won the starting spot.

I turned the Jeep around at the community college and came back on Third Avenue. When I saw the turn-off for Carkeek Park, all I was thinking about were the curves on the road going down. I pushed on the accelerator, taking each one as fast as I could, tires squealing in the summer heat. I didn't think about Piper's Creek until I reached the parking lot and saw it, right in front of me. I looked around. No police. I revved the engine, popped the clutch, bounced up and over the curb, and then roared down into the creek and up the other side, tires spinning but pulling me out and back onto the road.

12

SATURDAY I WENT to the gym early. I knew Peter would want to hear how I'd done. The sun was shining and a breeze was blowing in from the Sound. Popeye's was nearly empty—everybody was outside. I asked the guy behind the counter if Peter was around. "He said he was going to Jamba Juice. He's probably sitting on the steps leading down to the cut."

I walked toward the water and spotted him leaning against a cement block, watching the boats. "Hey," I said. "Got a minute?"

"Tell me," he said. "How'd it go?"

"I did it, Peter. I blew them away. I'm starting, and I feel so strong out on the field. So ready. I'm going to have a big year. I know it all through my body."

He reached and gave me a high-five. "I told you you'd rock and roll. Didn't I tell you?"

I nodded and then fell silent.

"So what else? I can tell there's more," he said.

"The season is starting now."

"So?"

"So this is when I stop using the steroids. Remember?"

"Yeah, yeah," he said. "I remember you saying something like that."

"What I'm wondering is, will you still train me?"

He smiled. "Ofcourse. I'll admit I've made a few extra bucks from the steroids, but it's not like I need that money to pay the rent. And your dad pays me for the one-on-one sessions. I just hope you know what you're doing."

"What's that mean?"

He looked out over the water. "Most guys don't go off the juice unless they have to. They don't drug test in high school, right? So why not do another stack? You see what it does for you, how strong it makes you. Why stop?"

"There are a bunch of reasons."

"Like?"

I paused. "It's hard to explain."

For a long time neither of us spoke. Then he held out his Jamba Juice cup toward me. "You want some mango smoothie?"

"Sure," I said.

I took a good swallow and handed the cup back to him. He stirred his straw around a few times. "We're sort of back to where we started, aren't we?" he said.

I nodded, then stretched my arms over my head and stood. "I'm going to work out now," I said and started toward the gym.

Once I was in the gym, I headed to the free weights area and lifted. It was the first time I'd lifted without the help of steroids in a long time. I hadn't been able to explain to Peter why I was quitting because I couldn't totally explain it to myself. What I'd done was cheating, but deep down I didn't think of myself as a cheater. I'd gotten on the train for a while, just to get a boost, just to get that starting spot. But now that I had it, it was going to be *me* that was keeping it, not some drug. And there was more. By stopping, I could look Drew in the eye again without feeling like a liar, and that mattered a lot. Maybe I could even get things going with Kaylee. People become alcoholics or drug addicts, and then they stop and nobody holds it against them. It was the same with me. I'd used steroids, but I'd stopped.

I wasn't proud of what I'd done; I wouldn't want anybody to ever find out; but the important thing was that
it was in the past.

. . .

The rest of the summer went by in a flash. Football
practice . . . chores for my dad . . . weightlifting. I kept
working out at Popeye's, kept getting help from Peter.
I wasn't setting any new personal records, but I wasn't
dropping off much from my highs. I could do it. I could
do it on the up-and-up; I could do it right.

PART FIVE

1

OUR OPENER WAS AT HOME ON a Friday night against the Franklin Quakers at Memorial Stadium. Franklin is good at soccer, they're good at tennis, and they're great at basketball, but at football they suck. They've got sixteen hundred kids, same as every school in our league, but their best athletes never go out for football.

Friday after school we had a short meeting. Carlson went over the defensive game plan first: lots of zones, not much blitzing. Finally he turned to the offense. "We're going to run Mick at them until they prove they can stop him. Linemen, block straight ahead. Nothing fancy—just find the closest guy and knock him on his ass. Mick, keep your head up, look for a hole, and then explode into it. Drew, no audibles. I don't want to see the ball in the air unless I call for a pass play."

Drew nodded.

"All right, then. One final thing. We are playing smash-mouth, in-your-face football. But smash-mouth football is not dirty football. We are the Shilshole

Raiders, not the Oakland Raiders. You hear the whistle, you stop. No cheap shots, ever. Understood?" He paused, looking us over. "Come tonight with your A game."

When I pulled onto our street, I saw my dad's pickup in the driveway. He opened the front door as soon as he saw the Jeep. "I took the day off," he said. "I wouldn't have been able to concentrate anyway. How you feeling? You nervous? You want to practice anything?"

I was glad to have a way to get rid of the two hours. We went to Crown Hill Park and tossed the ball around just enough for me to break a light sweat. At five o'clock we headed back to the house. At five-thirty, I was driving down Fifteenth toward Memorial Stadium.

I was nervous in the locker room. I looked around at the other guys, and they were feeling it, too. Before every game, you worry that some guy on the other team is going to manhandle you, humiliate you, show you up. Everybody talks big, but the fear of failure is as close and tight as your helmet.

Carlson's pregame talk was no different from those of any coach I've ever had. When he finished, he looked at his watch and then looked at us: "All right, men, time to take the field." We ran through the tunnel screaming, trying to fight back our fear with noise.

We won the coin toss and took the kickoff. Carlson had thrown Dave Kane a bone, making him our return man on punts and kickoffs. Kane ran the ball out to the thirty-five, giving us good field position. As soon as the whistle blew, ending the play, I trotted out with Drew and DeShawn and the rest of the offense, trying to do everything slowly because inside everything was racing fast.

Carlson had me running out of the I formation, which I prefer to any split-back formation. I like to get the ball deep in the backfield, stretch the defense as I take my first couple of steps looking for a hole, and then go.

We started the way Carlson had said we would—a run straight up the middle. I took Drew's handoff, saw a glimmer of a hole between Tyler Ashby and our center Dan Driessen, and made my move. I hit that hole hard and fast, was through it before I felt contact, and then burst into the secondary. Some Franklin guy took my legs out from under me and I went down hard, but I had gained eight yards. I bounced up and hustled back to the huddle.

"Thirty-four delay. On one."

After the snap, I waited two beats. Drew pretended to be dropping back to pass and then slipped the ball to my gut. This time the hole was outside our left guard. I drove into that opening, no fancy moves, and I gained another six yards. "First down!" the referee called.

All it took was a handful more plays. A toss sweep, a delay, another toss sweep, and then a counter that I cut back against the grain for the final thirty-four yards. Four Franklin guys took shots at me on that last run, but not one could bring me down. Over the loud-speaker I heard the magic words: "Mick Johnson scores a touchdown for Shilshole."

Drew was there to high-five me, and so were DeShawn and the other guys. We trotted as a group back to the sidelines. I took a couple sips of water and then heard a huge cheer from the student section be-hind me. Franklin had fumbled the kickoff. "Go! Go!" Carlson was shouting. "Offense on the field!"

I pulled my helmet over my head and raced onto the field. "Thirty-four sweep left, on one," Drew called out. Five seconds later I was breaking into the open field again, and ten seconds later the PA announcer was say-ing, "Mick Johnson scores a touchdown for Shilshole."

That's how it went, drive after drive. I ran and ran, scoring twice in the second quarter and once more in the third. I was sure Carlson would yank me when the score reached 28–0, but he kept the first team in, on both offense and defense. I scored the last touchdown of the game on a sixty-yard run with a minute left. That touchdown pushed the score to 48–0.

In the locker room afterward, guys pounded me on the back, hollering that I was all-world. I was smiling so hard, my cheeks hurt. In the middle of the celebration, Carlson called me into the office. I thought he'd be beaming, but his eyes were serious. "You're going to read all about yourself in the paper tomorrow. You set a bunch of records today. Touchdowns, yards gained—all sorts of records."

"The blocking was great," I said. "It was the line that did everything."

Carlson shook his head. "Our line was good, not great. You did what you did because Franklin was terrible."

I stood silent, not sure what he wanted.

"I don't like running up the score, and I don't believe in individual records. I let you rack up all those yards and touchdowns because I want the rest of the teams in the league—Inglemoor and Eastlake and especially Foothill—I want them to see the score and wonder about us, maybe even fear us. You understand?"

I nodded. "I understand."

"Good, because the one thing I don't want is for you to think you're Walter Payton just because you're wearing his number. Clear?"

"Clear."

"All right then, get back out there with your teammates."

When I returned to the locker room, the craziness was ending and the exhaustion was setting in. Guys were sitting on benches, pulling off their shoes and undoing their shoulder pads. I went from lineman to lineman, patting them on the back and thanking them for all their blocks. Each of them looked up at me, tired but happy, just like I was.

It wasn't until I got home that I even thought about the steroids. I'd stopped using them, but weren't they still in my blood and in my muscles? How much of what I'd done was me and how much them? I'd never know for sure. But there was one thing I did know—with every tick of the clock, I was moving closer to the day when I'd be entirely on my own. It was a good feeling, but it was a scary feeling, too.

2

WHEN I STEPPED OUT OF BED Saturday morning, I expected to have to crawl to the bathroom. All those carries meant that many hits, and a running back pays for every hit with an ache somewhere. I'm not saying I didn't hurt at all, because I did, but the pain wasn't half as bad as I'd expected.

I went downstairs to eat. My dad was sitting at the table, waiting for me. Next to my cereal bowl was the *Seattle Times*. He had it opened to the high school sports page. The headline jumped at me.

Mick Johnson Runs Wild

Below the headline, in smaller type, were the words

Record-Shattering Performance

"Read it," he said. "Go ahead."

I read the article and then reread it. I'd gained three hundred twelve yards and had scored six touchdowns. The list of school records I'd set or tied made me woozy: *Most yards in a game. Most touchdowns in a game. Most yards per carry.*

"You're on your way," my dad said. "You back up this game with more big games and by the end of next year, every college coach in the country will know your name." He paused. "Who do you play next?"

"Garfield."

"Are they any good?"

"Their offense is, but their defense is weak. They beat Roosevelt forty-one to thirty-three."

He smiled. "Sounds like the perfect team to play. Keep it rolling."

. .

At school everybody had heard about the records, and it changed the way people looked at me. Before the Franklin game, I was just another jock. Now kids—and even teachers—went out of their way to say hello. Right before lunch, I met Kaylee in the hall. "You were great, Mick," she said. "You were amazing. Did you see me waving to you? I was just to the left of the band."

"Yeah, I saw you," I said, afraid to tell her I'd been so focused on the game that I hadn't once looked up into the stands.

During lunch a reporter from the school newspaper interviewed me. I felt like an NFL pro, answering questions about how it felt to hold records. I even answered like an NFL pro, saying stuff like "Records are meant to be broken." And "It's really a tribute to my linemen." At the end of the interview, the school photographer snapped a photo.

After school, as I was heading to the football field, I heard my name shouted. I turned. It was Natalie Vick. "Girls' volleyball season starts tonight," she said, an edge to her voice.

"I saw that," I said.

"Kaylee's on the team. She's the only sophomore."

"That's great," I said. "Good for her."

"She's a starter." She stood, hands on her hips. "So will you be at the game?"

I wasn't expecting the question. "Maybe. But I've got practice, and then I go to the gym for weight—"

"You are so stupid, Mick," Natalie said, interrupting. "Do you have a clue what a great person Kaylee is? Every guy in this school wishes he was in your shoes."

"What about Brad? I thought she was with him."

"Are you really that dense? We needed somebody for volleyball when you stopped coming, so I called Brad. Kaylee doesn't like him, not the way she likes you, anyway. But she's not going to go chasing after you, Mick. She was at your football game, cheering for you. Now it's your turn."

"I'll be there," I said. A door had opened that I'd assumed was closed. "I promise you. I will be there."

All through practice, Carlson was watching me extra closely, looking for any sign that I had a big head, so I busted my gut on all the drills. A couple of times he nodded to me, and at the end he singled me out. "Way to work, Mick."

When practice ended, I called the house and left a message saying I was going to the volleyball game and wouldn't be home until late. Then I grabbed a sandwich at Subway and headed straight to Popeye's to get my workout done, because I wasn't skipping that.

When I walked into Popeye's, Peter held up the high school sports page from the *Seattle Times.* "Way to go, Mick!" he said, and the guys behind the counter and the lifters in the gym clapped for me.

He took me to the trainers' room for a free massage. I'd always thought massages were for rich women vacationing in Arizona. This massage was nothing like that. The massage guy would find tight muscles and then knead them until they came loose. It hurt almost as much as lifting, but when he finished I felt a thousand times better.

After that, Peter led me through a long stretching session, focusing on my back and my legs. Then he gave me a spreadsheet of my workouts for the week.

They were both shorter and easier than they'd been. I asked him why. "The games will take a lot out of you," he said. "And remember, you're off the juice."

"But I have to keep strong."

"Mick, trust me. This will be plenty."

I took the paper from him and headed out onto the gym floor. For the first time, I didn't follow what he'd written. The drops were too great; I wasn't going to give up so quickly. If he had me lifting one fifty for something, I pushed it to one sixty. If he had me doing fifteen reps, I forced myself to do eighteen. And I did it, too. I don't know that I've ever worked harder or longer, but I did it.

I didn't finish until nearly eight-thirty, and by then the place had emptied. As I toweled off, Peter came over. "I know you want to stay clean," Peter said, his voice a whisper. "But there's some new stuff I got a hold of. It's called XTR. That guy in the Tour de France—not Lance Armstrong but the guy after him, the guy who had the title taken away—it's what people think he used. He was way behind, he gave himself an injection of this stuff, and he won the thing. It would be perfect for a sport like football—it would give you power right on game day, when you most needed it."

"Not interested," I said. "No more steroids."

"Right, right, right," he said. "And I respect that one

hundred percent. I just wanted you to know about this stuff."

"Okay, you told me."

. . .

I went out to the Jeep, my stomach in knots. I'd lied—I *was* interested in the new stuff. But then I thought, *What athlete wouldn't be?* If Drew heard about it, or DeShawn, their eyes would light up, too. Being interested doesn't mean you are going to use it.

I started up the Jeep. The clock lit up—eight-forty-five. Suddenly I panicked: the volleyball match. If it was a blowout, the whole thing could be over before I made it back to school.

I shoved the Jeep into gear and headed straight to Shilshole High, driving fast. I had to catch at least the last game. If I could see Kaylee play, then I'd have something to talk to her about, and if I started talking to her, there was a chance we could get back to where we'd been in the summer.

When I pulled into the school parking lot, the gym doors were shut. I parked in a bus zone, jumped out of the Jeep, and started to run to the gym. I was about halfway when the doors burst open and people started pouring out: the game was over. I spotted Drew and DeShawn. I was about to call out to them when Natalie turned toward me. Our eyes met and she turned away. My stomach dropped. She'd tell Kaylee I'd missed her game, and that would be that. The door would close again.

I dragged myself back to the Jeep, drove home, and went upstairs to my room. I wanted to get in bed and sleep, but when I stepped inside the door, I saw a note pinned to the bulletin board above my desk. "Check out the den. Dad."

I turned around, went back down two flights of stairs, opened the door to the den, and flicked on the light. For a second I didn't notice anything. But then I saw it: the *Seattle Times* article framed and hung in the center of one of my walls. It wasn't bare anymore.

What happened next, I can't explain. It was like what had happened the day before tryouts, only worse. A huge lump came to my throat and my whole body started to shake. I wanted to bawl like a baby; I wanted to crawl into a hole and never come out.

You've got to fight through it. That's what Peter had said. I climbed back to my room and took a shower. At first all I could think was how unfair it was. I'd quit using steroids—why was the black hole still there? Then the warm water settled me; the shaking stopped and the lump in my throat went away, or at least it went down. I climbed into bed, flicked off the light, pulled the blankets over my head, and—after turning this way and that way over and over—fell asleep. When I awoke the next morning, I lay still for a moment, afraid, but the darkness was gone.

3

WITH THE SEASON under way, Carlson had fewer full-contact practices, and the ones we had were short. Some guys complained, but he waved them off. "Remember, the idea is to hit the other guy, not one another. Save your energy for Garfield."

After practice I'd drive to Popeye's, wanting to work myself hard to keep myself strong. Every day I tried to do more than Peter had laid out for me. Finally he caught on. "I want to lift close to what I was lifting before," I explained. "Otherwise I'm going to drop off too fast."

He frowned. "Mick, you're going to drop off. It has to happen. If you don't adjust the weights, you're going to hurt yourself. If you want another trainer, that's okay. I'll find somebody for you. But if you want me, then you've got to follow my instructions. I do not let my clients injure themselves."

I didn't want to believe him, but after a while, I had no choice. Every time I tried to match a personal record, my muscles would start twitching and I'd feel as if they were going to explode.

You see yourself go downhill in one thing, and you can't help but be afraid you're headed downhill in everything. I told myself that the drop-offs were nothing to worry about, that they were too small to mean anything. I was a player, and nothing could change that. To build up my confidence, I went back in my mind and relived my best games in junior football. Then I jumped to the future: I pictured myself breaking free against Garfield, cutting through a hole and seeing nothing but daylight in front of me. And that visualization worked. For hours it worked. At the end of the day, though, I'd lie down in my bed and flick off the light, and with the darkness the questions came back.

That week took forever, but finally it was Friday. At practice all week Carlson had said one thing: "We've got to contain their quarterback." Garfield's quarterback was Rashard Braxton; USC was recruiting him, and so were Miami and Notre Dame. He ran onto the field like an NFL star—helmet off, black dreadlocks flowing behind him. Still, no player can win a football game by himself, and Garfield's offensive linemen looked undersize. I didn't see how Braxton could do much, not with those little guys blocking for him.

On the opening plays, our defensive ends broke through the Garfield line as if they were playing a JV team. They sacked Braxton on first down. On second down, he hurried a short pass in the flat to his tailback that fell incomplete. That made it third down and fifteen yards for a first. Carlson blitzed the middle linebacker, and our right defensive end beat his guy. It looked certain that Braxton would be sacked for a huge loss, but he ducked under the linebacker, shook off the end, and scrambled to his right.

He pump-faked, freezing the secondary, and then took off. Once he was in the open field, I saw what worried Carlson. Braxton was fast and he had size. Six guys must have had a shot at bringing him down, but none so much as laid a hand on him. Officially he ran eighty-three yards for a touchdown, but he must have covered close to a hundred eighty-three to get there.

Garfield 7, Shilshole 0.

Kane took the kickoff out to the twenty-eight. I pulled my helmet on and raced out to the huddle. I was pumped, wanting to shed my doubts by breaking a big play right out of the gate. But being too high can be as bad as being flat. My first rushing attempt was a simple run off tackle. Drew's handoff was good, but I took off before I got the ball properly tucked away. I was bobbling it when a Garfield guy smacked into me, and the ball squirted out. A cornerback dropped on it, and they were back in business inside our thirty.

I returned to the sidelines and stood as far away from everyone as I could, trying to calm myself. The other guys were all screaming: "Stop them! Stop them!" but I didn't say a word. I had to stop the voices in my own head.

Braxton took the snap, dropped back, and then broke straight upfield on a quarterback draw. He was past our linemen in a flash, made one cut to the right, and then was in the open field again. He made it to the three-yard line before he was brought down. Two plays later, Garfield led 13–0.

Up and down our sidelines, guys were sitting on the bench, elbows on their knees, shoulders slumped. Carlson saw it; he walked the length of the bench. "Stand up!" he shouted. "Keep your heads in the game. This thing has just started." Guys pulled themselves up and even cheered as Garfield kicked off, but when Dave Kane stumbled on the twelve-yard line and went down, untouched, on the fifteen, the cheers died away.

I trotted back onto the field. This was a crucial drive, for the team and for me.

The fast start had Garfield's defensive guys pumped up. On first down, Drew bobbled the snap and fell on the ball. Loss of two. On second down, I took a toss sweep and managed about six yards before I was swarmed under. That set up third and six.

The call was the toss sweep again. Drew looked at me and said, "Get the first down, Mick." I took his pitch and raced for the corner, looking for a place to cut back, but they kept stringing me out. Finally I cut up-field and picked up five yards before my legs were chopped out from under me, a yard short.

Drew unsnapped the buckle on his helmet and headed for the sidelines. I did the same. Fourth down deep in our own territory—there was nothing to do but punt. That's what I thought, but it's not what Carlson thought. Before we reached the bench, he called time-out. Then he pointed for us to go back onto the field.

We were going for it.

Stupid football—that's what an expert would have said. But Carlson was sending two messages. The first was to me. He was telling me that he believed in me, believed I could get the tough yard, and that pumped up the whole team. The second—and it was my dad who explained it to me—was to the rest of the coaches in the league. They'd see the film, or at least hear what he'd done. He was showing them that when they played Shilshole High, they could expect the unexpected.

The play was a simple dive: 34 right on two. The Garfield defense was up close, eleven guys within three yards of the line of scrimmage, all of them trying to shut me down. Drew took the snap, spun, and stuck the ball in my gut. Ashby had fired off the line and had smacked his man, pushing him back and off to the right. I burst through that hole, felt somebody's hands slide off me, and then I was in the open field. With the entire defense up close, Garfield had nobody back. I looked over my shoulder at the forty and saw one of their cornerbacks gaining on me. It was a footrace. I headed toward the right corner of the end zone, forcing him to run and run to catch me, and when I looked back again, he was pulling up, letting me go. Seventy-six yards for the touchdown.

When I crossed the goal line, I felt like a jet breaking through low clouds and coming out into the blue skies of the upper atmosphere. I'd done it. On my own, in the clutch, I'd broken a big play.

The touchdown turned the game around. After that, we were the team that was pumped; Garfield was the team in a state of shock. Rashard Braxton kept running like a man possessed—reversing his field, cutting this way and that, doing everything for his team. But by the middle of the third quarter, he started wearing down, and by the fourth quarter, it was time to stick a fork in him—he was done.

By halftime I was drained, too, but I kept going. Sometimes I'd run a sweep; sometimes I'd run off tackle; sometimes I'd catch a little swing pass in the flat. Always I turned upfield and put a lick on somebody before I went down. Nothing came easy; I fought for every yard and every first down. At the start of the fourth quarter, Carlson pulled me and sent Kane in. Only then did I look at the scoreboard.

Shilshole 41, Garfield 20.

Other than the long run in the first quarter, I hadn't broken anything big. But in the locker room, Gabe Reese, our team manager, showed me the stat sheet. Three touchdowns and one hundred forty yards. "You've got eight touchdowns and over four hundred fifty yards for the season," Reese said. "That's more touchdowns than Drager scored all last season, and nearly as many yards."

When I got home, my dad and mom were sitting in the kitchen, waiting for me. My dad had gone to Just Desserts, a super-fancy chocolate place near Seattle

Center, and had bought three slices of cake. "I should have done this last week," he said. "I was just so excited, I didn't think."

I was tired and sore, but I was also starving. While I washed the cake down with an ice-cold glass of milk, my dad described the game to my mom. He remembered every play I'd made, every tackle I'd broken. It was as if he'd memorized the game, or at least had memorized my part of the game. "You really should come, Patti," he said. "Your son is a thing of wonder."

My mom smiled. "You know how I feel about that. Hearing about it is great. Seeing it?" She shook her head.

. . .

The next morning the newspaper was right by my breakfast plate. The headline was a little smaller, but it was still a headline.

Johnson Leads Shilshole over Garfield

The writer said that I'd followed up my record-setting performance with another outstanding effort. Then he quoted the Garfield coach. "The Johnson kid was the difference. He's fast and he's powerful. We just didn't have an answer."

4

I GOT A BUNCH of congratulations again on Monday at school, but there were fewer than the week before. Part of me was disappointed, but in another way it was good. That black hole was always in the back of my mind. If I could keep myself from climbing too high, then it might keep me from dropping too low.

We had a light practice, the lightest ever. Shorts, no pads, hardly any time with the helmet on. It was all timing and execution. Carlson had us walk through the plays, then we'd go half speed, then full speed. "Everything crisp, everything precise, every time." That was Carlson's challenge.

As I was changing after practice, Mr. Stimes, the trainer, came over.

"Got a minute, Mick?" he said as I laced up a shoe.

"I guess, but I got to go pretty quick."

"This won't take long. I'll be in the trainers' office."

I finished lacing my shoes, grabbed my duffel, and walked to his office. Stimes waved me in. As soon as I sat down, he picked up a clipboard. "I've been entering the data from the tryouts into a spreadsheet for Coach Carlson. As I was typing in the numbers, that forty-yard dash of yours caught my eye. I decided to go back and retrieve your stats from last spring, and then compare them with the August numbers. That got me looking at some of your other numbers." He stopped looking at the clipboard and instead looked at me. "I discovered some interesting things. Amazing things, actually."

"Like what?" I said.

"Like you've gained twenty-one pounds since June. Like you bench-press seventy-five pounds more. Like you're two seconds faster in the agility drill. You squat one hundred ten pounds more." He paused. "Frankly, I've never seen anything like it. It's as if you've become a different person."

I kept my eyes down. "I worked out every day over the summer, just like Coach wanted us to. It paid off."

"Where did you work out?"

I almost lied, but then I realized Stimes might have talked to Drew or DeShawn. "At Popeye's. It's a gym on—"

"I know where it is," he said. "How did you end up there?"

"My dad's business. He gets a free family member-ship. My dad used to play for the—"

"I know all about your dad," Stimes said. "I want to know about you and Popeye's."

I looked out the glass window. My heart was pound-ing and I could feel the blood flowing to my face. It was a nightmare. All the time I'd been using, nobody had suspected. Now I'd stopped, now I was clean, and Stimes was circling in.

"There's nothing to know," I said evenly, choosing every word carefully. "My dad arranged for me to have a personal trainer. Nothing against Coach Carlson, but the trainer had me lift differently, with better equipment, and it worked. I got bigger. My dad had the same sort of growth spurt when he was my age. He wasn't that big as a freshman, but then between his freshman and sophomore years, he took off, and he ended up in the NFL. I'm his son. So, you know, genetics and all that. You can ask him if you want. He'll tell you." I stopped, aware I was talking too much. That's what liars always do: talk too much.

Stimes interlaced his fingers and rested his chin on them. "Your trainer at Popeye's. Does he have you taking anything?"

"What do you mean?"

"You know what I mean. Pills. Anything like that."

"I take vitamins and drink a protein shake, but not because of the trainer at Popeye's. I found out about that on my own. All I do at Popeye's is lift. They've got cables and Smith machines and—"

"Mick, are you on steroids?"

I made myself look him in the eye. "No way, Mr.

Stimes. I'm not," I said. It was the truth. But somehow it didn't feel like the truth.

For a long moment, neither of us spoke. Then I stood "I've got to go," I said, and started for the door. I'd opened it and had one foot out when Stimes's voice stopped me.

"What's the name of your trainer?"

"My trainer?"

"Yeah, your trainer. What's his name?"

"Peter."

"Last name?"

I screwed up my face. "I'm not really sure. Walsh, or something like that. I just call him Peter."

5

ONCE I WAS AWAY from Stimes, I drove straight to Popeye's. I walked through the gym, searching for Peter. When I couldn't find him, I started my regular workout, doing lifts for the lower body. As I worked, I kept looking for him. He had to hear about Stimes.

Forty minutes went by, then fifty, then an hour. I walked to the main desk, where a guy with about forty earrings was reading *Body Builder* magazine. "Peter coming today?" I said.

He turned and shouted to someone in the back. "Did Peter quit?"

"No. At least, not yet."

The earring guy turned back to me. "I don't know where he is."

I returned and tried to do my squats, but my head was reeling. What would I do if Peter left? He was more than my trainer; I trusted him, as a friend. He knew everything and nobody else did.

I lifted for ten more minutes. Finally, just when I'd decided to leave, Peter strode through the door. He waved to me, and I motioned for him to come over. "What's up?" he said, smiling.

"You're not quitting, are you?"

His eyebrows went up. "Is that what they said?" He shook his head. "I just had an argument with the owner. And if I ever did quit this place, I'd still be around. All Fitness up in Shoreline has been after me for a year."

I took a deep breath, relieved. "Listen, probably nothing will happen, but . . ."

As I described what had happened with Stimes, Peter's face soured. "Do you think he'll come here?"

"I doubt it," I said. "Teachers always talk about making calls, but they hardly ever do it."

Peter chewed on his lip for a little. "It's illegal in Washington to test high school athletes for drugs. That means he could never prove anything unless you said something."

"I wouldn't say anything. You know I wouldn't."

He pointed his finger at me, and his face was different, almost menacing. "You'd better not, Mick. It would be worse for you than for me. All those dreams about going on to college and the NFL and all that. You get nailed with a steroid rap and you can kiss them goodbye. You'd never play anywhere, not even at Southeast Louisiana Junior College."

"I told you I wouldn't say anything."

The look stayed on Peter's face. "And don't tell any of your friends what you've done. Not a word to anybody, ever."

"I haven't told anybody and I never will."

"Okay," he said, but there was still anger in his voice.

I left then, feeling confused. I don't know what I'd expected from Peter, but it hadn't been what I'd gotten—his distrust.

I drove home, ate the steak dinner my mom made for me, and then started up the stairs to my room. I'd taken a couple of steps when I reversed myself and went down to the den. Sure enough, there was the second article, framed, hanging next to the first.

I heard footsteps and turned to see my mom. She came and stood by me. "I'm proud of you, Mick." She gestured toward the articles. "I know how hard you've worked to accomplish all this. I'm very, very proud."

. . .

The following school day went along like most school days. Practice was the same, except the whole time I kept sneaking looks at Stimes, afraid of what he might be thinking. Nothing happened on the field, though, and nothing happened in the film room. After practice, as I was heading out, Drew called out to me. "Hey, Mick, wait up." I stopped, and he caught up to me. "So, you going to Heather's birthday party?"

The invitation had come a week earlier—she was having a swimming party at Green Lake pool. After I'd opened it, I'd shoved it in a drawer, undecided what to do. Part of me wanted to go so that I could try somehow to make things right with Kaylee. But another part of me wanted to let all that go, at least until football season was over.

"I don't know," I said.

"Why not? It'll be fun."

"I'm not that big on swimming."

Drew's voice went low. "Is it the acne, Mick?"

"What?" I said, startled.

"Your acne," he repeated. "That's why you stopped

going to Green Lake in the summer, isn't it? You were afraid we'd want to go swimming and you'd have to take your shirt off and Kaylee would see your zits."

I reddened. "I have no clue what you're talking about, Drew."

"Just listen to me, Mick. Okay? And don't get mad. My dad had bad acne. He's always been afraid that I'd get it, too. And I started to, last year. But the thing is, there's medication now. He took me in and I take these pills and they work. Just get your parents to take you to your doctor, or go on your own."

As he spoke, all the shame I'd felt on the pier came back. Right after, the anger came, too.

"Say something, Mick," Drew said at last.

"I've already taken care of it, Drew," I answered, my voice cold. "All my zits are gone. If you'd like me to take my shirt off for you, I will."

"Forget I said anything, Mick. Okay?"

I took a deep breath. "Okay."

He looked me in the eye. "I was just trying to be a friend," he said.

"I know," I said, suddenly realizing he was my only real friend.

6

OUR NEXT THREE GAMES were against Roosevelt, Inglemoor, and Juanita—the weakest teams in the league. When I saw them on the schedule, I started picturing the long runs I'd make against them. But before the Roosevelt game, Carlson called me into his office. "I'm going to cut back on the number of carries you get for a few games, Mick," he said. "I'm going to open up the passing game more, run Kane out there to give you a breather. You're still our number one running back. I just don't want to wear you out." It was the exact strategy Downs hadn't used the year before.

"Coach," I said, "I'm not wearing out at all. I feel great. I can carry the ball as much as you want. I get stronger as the game goes on."

He drummed his fingers on the top of his desk and then slid a piece of paper to me. "There's your breakdown, quarter by quarter, for the Garfield game." I looked at the sheet. In the first quarter, I'd gained ninety-two yards. In the second it was thirty-one. In the third only seventeen.

"But that's because the game changed," I protested. "We got ahead and—"

"Mick," Carlson said, "you'll play when I say."

When I complained to my dad, he shut me down. "Smart coach," he said. "After your fast start, every team you face will be scheming to stop you. Drew clicks on a few touchdown passes to DeShawn, they'll be forced to drop the linebackers and safeties back a few steps, and that should open up things for you. And letting that other kid take some hits, that won't hurt you late in the season."

It all made sense, but one thing clouded the picture: those yardage stats. I hadn't known I'd dropped off so dramatically. Tuesday at the tail end of practice, we watched the game films. Guys all cheered my big touchdown run, but after that it was a grind-it-out game. I studied my own performance. As the game progressed I wasn't as quick off the snap, not as fast to the corners. On a couple of plays, there'd been gaping holes that somehow I'd missed, instead running right into tacklers. When the film session was over, I was too quiet and Drew noticed. "What's eating you?"

"You saw the films. After the first quarter, I did nothing."

"What are you talking about? You got the hard yards, Mick. The first downs on third and two. They knew we weren't passing; they were keyed entirely on you. So you didn't break any long ones. So what? You're the league's leading rusher; you're playing on an unbeaten team. Enjoy it."

That made me feel better, but I was determined to make the most of my chances against Roosevelt. I worked hard at practice and hard at Popeye's after practice. I wanted to break a couple long runs.

Sometimes, though, the harder you try, the worse you do. That's what happened against Roosevelt. I kept running into my blockers or tripping over defenders or taking the ball outside when I should have cut it back against the grain. I had eleven carries for forty-seven yards, and my longest run was a paltry eight yards. I did score a touchdown, and we did win 27–6, but the feeling afterward was nothing like it was the first two games, and there were no headlines in the paper.

Carlson didn't say anything—good or bad—about my performance, but my dad did. "You looked sluggish out there."

"I just never found my rhythm," I said.

He nodded. "Yeah, I know the feeling. It's hard to get up for a bad team. You'll break one next week."

But it was more of the same against Inglemoor. Drew and DeShawn clicked big-time, so we won 48–6. I carried the ball nine times for forty-six yards. Nothing wrong with those stats, but nothing particularly right about them, either.

The Inglemoor game was on Saturday night. Sunday morning I drove to Popeye's. Peter was there, and he gave me a quick wave, but he didn't come over to ask how I'd played. I went to the cables and started to do some curls, but my shoulders hurt and so did my back. Nine carries—and I ached all over.

Peter was working with Paul Krause, a guy in his late twenties. Most lifters who used steroids were secretive about it, but not Krause. I'd heard him talk about his favorite drugs as if he were describing toppings for a pizza. Now he was standing in front of the mirror, bench-pressing two hundred pounds in perfect rhythm: inhaling, exhaling—his arms moving from flexed to straight to flexed. He would work for another hour, and tomorrow he wouldn't hurt like I hurt.

The first time the D-bol had kicked in, I'd felt strong—just like Krause felt strong. And as those weeks rolled by, I'd just kept feeling stronger, which was the opposite of what was happening to me now, when with every passing day I felt weaker. The temptation was right in front of me. I could walk over to Peter, talk to him for thirty seconds, and pay him his money. Within a week the steroids would be working their magic. I'd be back on the train; I'd be stronger and faster—with less pain.

I looked around, feeling panicked. I had to get away, and I had to get away fast. I stopped right in the middle of a set, dropped the weights, walked out of Popeye's, and got into the Jeep. I started it up and then sat, engine idling. Where was I going? What was I going to do?

I pulled out my cell phone and punched in Drew's number.

"How you feeling?" I said when he answered.

He groaned. "How do you think? I'm sore all over."

I laughed a little. "Me, too. But I'm also bored out of my mind. You want to do something—maybe miniature golf?"

"I'll tell you what I want to do. I want to lie in bed all day long with a heating pad taped to my ribs. I think every single one of them is broken."

"Come on, Drew."

"I'm in serious pain here. I don't feel like doing anything."

After I closed my cell phone, I sat looking out at the Fremont Bridge. There was no one else I could call. That's when my cell phone rang. I flipped it open. "All right," Drew said. "Miniature golf it is. I'll meet you in half an hour at Interbay. But you're probably going have to take the ball out of the hole for me. I don't think I can bend."

"No problem," I said. "Glad to do it. See you in half an hour." I shut the phone and then leaned my head against the steering wheel and closed my eyes. He'd save me from myself; I could breathe again.

. . .

That week I took a different approach. I did everything I could to conserve my energy, to save every ounce of strength for the game. Instead of working super hard at Popeye's, I cut back, using lighter weights and concentrating more on stretching out my muscles than building them up.

I needed a good game Friday night against Juanita. I needed it for my confidence, and I needed it to give Carlson confidence in me. Everything he'd said after the Inglemoor game was positive, but I knew what was happening. Dave Kane was playing better and better every week. His star was shining brighter and mine was fading. Instead of being the number one option in the offense, I'd become just one of the options.

In the warm-ups before the game, I tried to judge my readiness. Were my legs strong? Was my first step explosive? Was I mentally ready? I thought so, but I'd thought so when we'd played Roosevelt and Inglemoor.

We won the toss and took the opening kickoff. Our first two plays were passes, and both of them were completions—one to Bo Jones and the other to DeShawn. I was figuring on another pass play, but Drew leaned forward and said the magic words: 34 draw on three.

Juanita came with the blitz. Drew sold the pass perfectly and slipped the ball into my arms, and I was past the first wave of defenders before they even knew it was a running play. My legs felt strong as I burst past the fifty-yard line. A linebacker was closing, but I dipped left, did a one-eighty-degree spin, and he missed me. A little stutter step followed by a quick burst took care of the safety, and I had enough speed to take it all the way to the end zone before the final cornerback reached me.

It was the shot of confidence I needed. As I crossed the goal line, all the clouds that had been hanging over me were blown away, just as I'd blown away that linebacker. I turned around, expecting to see my teammates streaking down the field toward me. Instead I saw the referee picking up the yellow penalty flag. The call was against us—holding.

The play was coming back; my touchdown was erased.

I should have shaken it off. Penalties are part of the game. You just go out there and do it again. It wasn't as if Juanita had a ferocious defense. No big deal—that's what I told myself. But after that play I couldn't get a spark. Instead of feeling fast and full of fight, I felt heavy and strangely unmotivated, almost as if I weren't really playing the game but was instead watching it from somewhere inside my head. I didn't stink up the place—ten carries, forty yards, one touchdown. Dave Kane carried the ball about the same number of times for the same number of yards, maybe a few more. We won the game 32–12, our fifth straight win—but my third straight mediocre game.

. . .

Heather's birthday party was the next day. I had told her I'd be there, and she said that Kaylee would be glad. That morning came up cold, gray, and blustery. I cleaned the gutters for my dad, which took a couple of hours. After lunch, I drove over to Popeye's, but instead of going in, I walked along the Fremont Cut, frozen to the bone by the sharp wind and the constant rain.

Was I just having a down time? Every player has

times when nothing seems to go right. Emmitt Smith, Walter Payton—all the great ones had lousy games. And I hadn't been that bad. I thought about the touchdown run that had been called back and how that might have changed everything for me. *Just hang in there,* I told myself. *Things have to start breaking my way. They just have to.*

I drove home. Heather's party started at six. Pizza, then swimming, then cake—why didn't it sound good? "Did you remember to buy Heather a gift?" my mom said as I headed out the door.

I hadn't. "There's a Starbucks across the street from the pool. I'll get her a gift card."

"Have fun."

I was halfway up Phinney Ridge when I remembered my swimsuit. It was wrapped up in a towel by the side of my bed. I turned on Greenwood and started to circle back, and then I just didn't want to do any of it—go back home, go to Starbucks, go to the swim party—nothing felt worth it.

Instead, I drove the Jeep out to I-5 and drove up to Bellingham, the whole time thinking about the new stuff, the XTR, Peter had told me about. If I did use it once, just to find out if it really worked, how bad would that really be? I didn't know what other guys were using. Number 50 from Foothill—Drew and DeShawn had been suspicious of him. They'd been suspicious of Foothill's whole team.

I stopped at a Starbucks in the Fairhaven neighborhood and had an Odwalla and a bagel, taking as long as I could, my mind going and going. Being a cheater—that's not how I wanted to think of myself. But I didn't want to be stupid, either. Guys used caffeine drinks all the time. Some guys even took caffeine pills. In one league a supplement would be legal; in another the same one would be banned. None of the rules made much sense when you stepped back and thought them through.

I stayed at Starbucks for about an hour. Afterward I found a Barnes and Noble and killed another hour looking at magazines, but really thinking the same thoughts. Instead of I-5, I took Chuckanut Drive home. As I drove along the Sound, a sudden fear chilled me. What if Drew called my house and asked where I was? I worried about that for ten miles or so, until it hit me that Drew didn't care much if I was there or not. I could picture him sitting by the pool with DeShawn. He'd be eating pizza and staring at the girls in their swimsuits. We'd been best friends once. That we weren't anymore was my fault.

When I got home, the house was dark. The next morning my mom asked how the party had been. "It was great," I said. "A lot of fun."

7

THE EASY PART of our season was over. Our next game was against Woodinville. They were 4-1, their only loss coming against Foothill on a last-second field goal. Beating them was going to require our best game of the year, especially since we were playing them on their field. Everybody knew the stakes, and the intensity picked up all week in practice. The coaches yelled more; guys scuffled more.

Early on at Thursday's practice, I saw Carlson talking on the sidelines with Dave Kane. Kane kept nodding his head, and at the end Carlson put his hand on Kane's shoulder pad and gave it a good shake. Kane hustled over to where I was. "Coach wants to talk to you," he said, a cockiness in his voice.

I made my way to Carlson. "All right, Mick, here's the deal. In the first half, you and Kane will split time at running back. He'll get the first quarter; you'll get the second. Whichever one of you has got the better feel for the game will play the second half. Neither one of you impresses me, then you'll alternate the second half, too." He paused. "No knock against you. Kane's been playing hard; he's earned this chance."

"I understand, Coach," I said calmly. But inside my head a buzz saw was roaring.

For the rest of that practice, Kane would run a series of plays with the first team and then stand back while I ran a series of plays. Nobody said anything to me, but I could feel what they were thinking: I was on my way out. That's what my dad would think, too.

When practice ended, the buzz saw was still going in my head. I drove straight to Popeye's, tracked down Peter, and pulled him off to the side. "That new stuff," I said, my voice anxious. "Do you still have some?"

"Yeah," he said. "I've got some in the back—"

"I want to try it," I said, interrupting. "Just to see."

"Hey, fine by me. I never understood why you stopped in the first place."

He led me into the conference room. "How many doses do you want? They're twenty-five bucks a shot."

"Just one."

"Mick, how many games you got left?"

"Four. More if we make the playoffs."

"Then I'm going to bring you four vials. Just pay for

one, and if you don't use the other ones, give them back to me. No charge. I don't want to be running back and forth handing you product every week. This is illegal, remember?"

He disappeared and came back a few minutes later with four small vials in his hand. I slipped him a twenty and a five. He stuck the money in his pocket, but he still kept hold of the vials. "This stuff is an amphetamine-steroid mix. You inject it and it goes to work almost immediately. Two to four hours—that's how long the effect lasts. All the things I warned you about—the 'roid rage, the depression—they come big-time with this. But the benefits are big-time, too."

When he finished, he slipped the vials to me. I stuck them into the small kit he'd given me when I'd started with the injections. I put the kit in the very bottom of my duffel bag and left.

As soon as I was outside, a crazy thing happened. Once I had the stuff, I decided I didn't really need it. I pictured Kane, pictured the way he ran with his blond hair flowing behind him. I was better than he was; I knew it in my heart. If Carlson wanted to see us head to head in a game situation, that was okay with me. I wasn't afraid to compete.

All Thursday and Friday I went back and forth. I'd

come up with five reasons that I should bring the XTR and then an hour later I'd think of five reasons that I shouldn't. I must have taken the kit out of my duffel and put it back in a dozen times.

Finally it was time to pack for the game. I had to decide. I knew the risk: If I got caught with a needle, that would be it for me, and not just for one year, but for my whole high school career. And if I couldn't play in high school, how could I ever get on a college team? But everything I'd done from those first D-bols on had been risky. The 'roid rage was a risk; the black hole was a risk. Going out and playing the game of football was a risk. I hadn't run all those risks to stand on the sidelines and watch Dave Kane play my position. I rolled up the kit in a small towel and shoved it deep into the duffel.

Because it was such an important game, Carlson insisted we all go on the team bus. As guys waited in the school parking lot, they dropped their duffels onto the sidewalk, but I kept mine tightly in my hand. And on the bus, instead of shoving it under my seat, I held it on my knees, close.

Once inside the locker room at Pop Keeney Field, I started to get into my gear. As I slid on my shoulder pads, all I could think about was the injection. When should I do it? Before Carlson's talk, or after? I kept putting it off and putting it off.

"All right, men," Carlson boomed out, and I moved toward him and listened as he gave his regular speech. When he finished, the guys turned and started to congregate at the mouth of the tunnel, their voices alive with excitement. The bathroom was empty. This was my chance, but before I could take a step Carlson yelled: "Let's go." Everybody started hollering and ten seconds later I was caught up with my teammates, charging through the tunnel and onto the field, screaming my lungs out, my duffel and the XTR back in the locker room.

The pregame warm-ups were like they always were, but when the horn sounded, signaling the start of the game, instead of feeling an adrenaline rush, I felt sick inside. It was Dave Kane who'd be taking the field, not me.

Then, just before the game started, Drew sidled up next to me. "Don't panic, Mick," he said. "You're better than Kane. I've seen you both run, and I know. You'll be fine."

Woodinville won the toss, but they deferred, which meant we'd have the ball first. Whenever a team does that, they're disrespecting you. They're saying, "We *know* our defense can stop your offense."

And they did. Drew's passing wasn't sharp, and the linemen were blowing blocking assignments, but it was Kane who was completely out of sync. On the first series, he was flagged for a false start, and then he broke the wrong way on a simple handoff, going to Drew's left side when Drew was looking for him on the right. On the second series, he dropped a swing pass and then had another false start.

I didn't need the XTR to outplay him; just a routine performance would have put him on the bench for the second half. But I didn't want to put him on the bench for the second half—I wanted him on the bench for the rest of the year, for the next two years. I wanted to grab my starting job back, grab it and hold it by the throat. I had to try everything, pull out all the stops. "Coach Carlson," I called. "I'm going into the locker room for a second. My stomach."

Carlson turned toward me. "Okay, but hustle."

I raced down the tunnel, grabbed my duffel, and headed to the bathroom. I stepped into the stall way in the back, pulled the door shut, and latched it. My hands were shaking so much that I dropped the syringe. It was plastic, so it didn't break, but for a second I wondered if somehow someone had seen it. A crazy thought—everyone else was on the field.

It had been nearly two months since I'd done an

injection, but it all came back. I used the isopropyl alcohol to clean my skin and the needle. Then I injected myself. Once the juice was in me, I cleaned the site again and massaged the muscle. I stuck the syringe and the vial back in the kit, wrapped the kit in the towel, and put it all at the bottom of the duffel. A minute later I was back on the sidelines.

"You okay?" Carlson said to me as he walked the sideline. "You're not too sick to play?"

"I'm fine," I said. "I can go in anytime."

Carlson stuck to his plan. Kane stayed out there the entire first quarter even though he scuffled on almost every play. Finally the quarter ended, and Carlson said the words I was waiting to hear: "All right, Mick. Get out there and do something."

Drew gave me a smile when I joined the huddle. "Counter thirty-four on two." He took the snap, pivoted, and then slipped me the ball. I cut inside and was by the Woodinville linemen before they knew I had the ball. I racked up twelve yards and a first down before being tackled. Next came a slant pass to Jones that clicked for six yards, but after that it was my number again, this time on a toss sweep that I broke back against the grain for fifteen yards. I wanted the ball again, but Carlson had Drew stretch the defense with a long bomb to DeShawn. The pass fell incomplete, and we came back with a screen pass to me. When I took in that pass and turned upfield, the guys in the Woodinville secondary were all ten yards off the line of scrimmage, afraid of being burned deep. Inside their forty-five, I gave their cornerback a hip fake, cut left, then immediately cut back to the right, leaving a second guy in my wake. After that I was in the open field and nobody was going to bring me down one-on-one. The guys that were faster than I was weren't strong enough, and the guys that were strong enough had no chance of catching me. It was as if I were going at full speed and they were all in slow motion.

"Touchdown Shilshole!" the public address announcer called once I crossed the goal line, and seconds later the guys swarmed me. After that touchdown, I raced to the sidelines. Carlson slapped me on the shoulder pads. I took a long swig of Gatorade, and then stood waiting, anxious. I figured our defense would stop them and then I'd go out there and score again and again and we'd have them buried by halftime.

Woodinville had other ideas.

After the kickoff, their offense came out firing on all cylinders, and it seemed that whatever defense Carlson called was the wrong defense. When we blitzed, their quarterback unloaded his passes quickly and accurately to a wide receiver. If we stayed back in a conventional defense, their running backs nickel-and-dimed us to death. Woodinville scored the tying touchdown on a bootleg by the quarterback. The guy could have walked in—that's how completely out of position our defense was. Woodinville had held the ball for what seemed like forever.

Once on ESPN I had seen an old Muhammad Ali–Joe Frazier fight in which those guys just stood toe to toe, exchanging punches. That's how the second quarter went. I stayed in the zone, knowing just when to go for the corner and just when to cut back, chewing up big chunks of yardage on nearly every carry. But everything I did, they matched. When the clock hit 00:00, ending the first half, the score was 14–14.

Carlson gave us a quick talk and then told us to rest. I was itching to get back on the field, but I looked around and saw all the guys with their heads down, wet towels around their necks, sucking air. Until that moment, I hadn't thought about the XTR. But once I saw how exhausted the other guys were, I knew the steroid buzz had kicked in. Not that I felt one hundred percent fresh—I didn't. I felt bruised and battered. But I knew from my teammates' eyes that I was stronger than they were, which meant that I was stronger than anybody on the Woodinville team, too.

I didn't play better in the third quarter. I had the same burst I had before, but everyone else had slowed a step, and some guys had slowed two. The six- and eight-yard gains I'd made in the first half were now ten- and twelve-yard gains. I was slicing through Woodinville like a sharp knife through a tender steak, cutting them into pieces. Carlson stopped pretending he was using the passing game. It was all me.

I kept pounding at them and pounding at them until, near the end of the third quarter, Woodinville cracked. I had six carries in a row, none of them for less than six yards. Instead of putting their bodies on the line to take their best shot at me, the linebackers and safeties were reaching out with their arms. When they finally did manage to bring me down, I'd pop up quickly to show them that I was still fresh. It was as if I were the Energizer Bunny, and they realized that nothing could shut me down. The drive ended when I took the ball eighteen yards straight up the gut and into the end zone, shedding tacklers the whole way. For the rest of the game, Woodinville's defense wanted no part of me. The 14–14 halftime tie turned into a 41–21 romp midway through the fourth quarter.

And then came what should have been the cherry on top of the ice cream. With one minute left in the game, I broke a ninety-four-yard touchdown run, cutting back twice and fighting off two tacklers at the ten-yard line. The league record for longest TD run was ninety-one yards. I knew because it was my dad who held it. As I crossed the goal line, I turned and looked back, expecting to see my teammates racing toward me. Instead, I heard the referee's whistle and saw him waving his arms, motioning for me to bring the ball back to the line of scrimmage.

A yellow penalty flag was lying on the ground.

I knew why. Out of the corner of my eye I'd seen DeShawn, split out ten yards and not even part of the play, move early. His penalty had wiped out my record-setting run.

At that instant, I wanted to get at DeShawn. I turned and started racing upfield toward him. I was going to smash him to the ground, pulverize him, and tear him to pieces the way a hurricane pulverizes a house.

But somewhere around the fifty-yard line, my brain clicked in. DeShawn's penalty didn't matter. We'd won. I was back in Carlson's good graces, both a starter and a star. I slowed, forcing myself to think, fighting the XTR, fighting the rage. My sprint turned into a run and

then a jog. By the time I reached the huddle I had myself under control.

On the ride back I sat right in the middle of the bus.
Sometimes three or four guys would talk to me at once,
telling me how great I'd played, how quick and fast and
powerful I'd been. I got punched in the shoulder so
many times that it hurt, but I didn't want the ride to end.

At home, my mom and dad were waiting for me.
"Where's that game been?" my dad asked when I
stepped through the door, a big smile on his face. I had
cake and ice cream and then went upstairs and showered. When I stepped out of the shower, I knew I was
still too wound up to sleep. I pulled on my jeans and
slipped downstairs, careful not to make a sound. I
started up the Jeep and headed into the night. The dark
was what I wanted, the soothing blackness of night.

I drove to Golden Gardens Park, parked the car, and
walked past the duck ponds and onto the beach. The
only light came from a sliver of a moon; I could barely
make out the white foam of the waves as they rolled in.
The waves were hypnotic; a thousand years ago they
had looked the same, sounded the same. A thousand
years from now they would look the same, sound the
same. I stared out at the water, wondering what it
would feel like to go out into it, go out and swim and

swim until you couldn't swim anymore, until the water swallowed you up.

I don't know how long I stood looking into the Sound. Finally a train whistled in the distance, and I turned and headed back to the car.

8

WITH THE WIN over Woodinville, it wasn't only the football team that was on a high—it was the whole school. I knew what would happen if I let myself get too high, so that whole week I kept to myself everywhere—in the classroom, on the practice field, in the gym.

It worked. I stayed on an even keel with no big highs or lows. Only one thing went wrong all week. After Thursday's practice, I was about to change into my street clothes when I remembered an elbow brace I'd left out on the field. Coach Carlson had wanted me to try it out but it had been too tight, so I'd thrown it off to the side. I trotted out to retrieve it and then brought it to the equipment room. When I returned to the locker room, I saw Drew rifling through my duffel bag. Instantly, my heart froze. The kit with the XTR and the syringe was still wrapped in a towel at the bottom.

"What are you doing, Drew?" I said, trying to keep my voice calm.

Drew held up his arm, showing me his forearm. It was raw, and the piece of gauze he had over the torn-away flesh was flapping free. "I'm getting tape to hold this on. You got tape, right?"

I reached over and pulled the duffel bag out of his hands. "I'll get it for you," I said. I was trying to be natural, but I pulled too hard.

Drew's eyes went wide and his face broke into a huge smile. "What are you hiding? You got a stack of *Playboy*s in there or something?"

Dan Driessen and Lee Choi and a bunch of other guys turned to look.

"I'm not hiding anything," I said.

"So what's the big deal?" Drew's voice wasn't so light.

"No big deal. I just don't like people going through my stuff."

I reached into my duffel, pulled out the tape, and tossed it to him. "There you go."

Drew caught the tape, peeled off a section, and then tossed it back.

9

GAME SEVEN WAS AGAINST Liberty High way out in Issaquah. They were good, but not great—the kind of team that could beat us only if we turned the ball over or committed a ton of penalties.

All week long I told myself I could play the game straight, that I didn't need anything, but on game day, I made sure the kit was in the bottom of my duffel.

Carlson had gotten a bus. On the ride out, I again held on tight to my duffel, trying not to look as though I was holding on tight. Every once in a while I'd glance at Drew and wonder if he suspected. Then I'd look at Stimes and think the same thing. Finally I realized how stupid I was being. They weren't thinking about me; they were thinking about the game.

The Liberty locker room was like every other one— dark, damp, and smelly. I sat down on one of the benches and got into my gear. Then I picked up my duffel and made my way to the bathroom, again choosing the stall farthest from the lockers. I thought I'd be less nervous, but my hands still shook. When I finished with the injection, I wrapped everything up in the towel, put it into the duffel, opened the stall door, stepped out, and looked back toward the locker room.

That's when I saw Drew. He was standing just inside the restroom door, about thirty feet away. For a moment we stared at each other, silent. "Let's crush these guys," he finally said.

I slung the duffel over my shoulder. "Okay by me," I answered, and I headed out to the locker room, my chest tight.

A couple minutes later, we huddled as a team at the mouth of the tunnel leading to the field. Around me guys were starting to scream and bounce up and down. The noise spread like a disease. An adrenaline-steroid-amphetamine craziness came over me, and pretty soon I was screaming and bouncing up and down more than anyone. The next thing I knew, I was running onto the field, then doing jumping jacks and pushups, and a few minutes later the game was on.

You play a team at their field, and it always takes time to get comfortable. I don't know why—a football field is a football field. We bumbled our way through the first quarter. I was too jumpy, too high, hitting the holes before the blocks had opened anything up. Drew turned the ball over on a fumbled snap, killing one drive, and another drive died when he tripped dropping back to pass.

Liberty had the ball near midfield at the start of the second quarter. I was standing along the sideline, wound tight as wire, watching our defense, when I felt someone staring at me. I looked, and as I did, Drew looked away. I went over to the trainer and got myself some water and then glanced back at him. Now he wasn't looking at me at all but was talking to DeShawn. They both laughed at something, then DeShawn gave Drew a push and Drew pushed him back. As I drank the water down, I told myself to stop imagining things.

Our defense held, and we were back on the field. We managed a couple of first downs before we had to punt. The whole game was stuck—neither team could do anything. Right before halftime, the Liberty kicker punched through a thirty-two-yard field goal. The ball actually hit the goalpost, but it flopped through on the opposite side, and those three points were the only points of the half.

During halftime, Carlson fumed. "You thought you were going to walk in here with your undefeated record and they were going to roll over for you, but they're not. I don't like losing when the other team is better, but I hate losing to a team that isn't as good. There's one reason they're ahead: they want it more than you. And they're going to beat you unless you turn it around. Now go out there and play some football."

For the rest of the break, the guys stretched out on

the benches, resting. But I was too keyed up to do that. I kept pacing back and forth. "Sit down, Mick," Middleton said. "You're making me tired."

I broke a few tackles on my first run of the second half, and then a few more tackles on the next run, and I could tell the Liberty defenders were back on their heels. We had the ball, second and four at their thirty-eight. I took Drew's handoff and worked my way toward the sideline, forcing them to pursue laterally. Driessen made a great block on their middle linebacker, and I cut upfield behind it. I had a full head of steam going as I broke into the secondary. A safety came up to try to tackle me, but I lowered my shoulder, sent him sprawling, and staggered toward the goal line before tumbling into the end zone for the first touchdown of the game. Shilshole 7, Liberty 3.

Liberty took the kickoff, but a holding penalty pushed them back into the shadow of their goalposts. Because of their terrible field position, they ran three straight running plays, and a bad punt gave us great field position. On first down, Carlson called the same stretch play again. I broke into the secondary, and there was that same safety coming up on me again. I'd embarrassed the guy the time before. He was a football player—he wanted to get revenge by laying a big hit on me, so I used that against him. Instead of taking him on, I juked left, took one step right, and then went left. He crossed his feet trying to stay with my move and then tripped and fell. I was by him like a flash. Shilshole 14, Liberty 3.

I thought we'd broken them. I thought our defense would hold them and that I'd be back on the field in minutes. I could hardly wait to get out there and crack that defense again, crack it the way you crack an egg against a pan.

But Liberty didn't quit. They slogged to a couple of first downs, and then, on a third and four near mid-field, they burned us with a trick play. It looked like their stock running play: a pitchout to their halfback sweeping right. The play developed slowly . . . too slowly. As our cornerback came up to tackle him, the halfback dropped back into a passing position. And there was Liberty's quarterback, streaking down the left side of the field, totally uncovered.

The halfback's pass was a wobbly spiral, but it led the quarterback perfectly. He caught the ball in stride and then raced down the sideline for their first touch-down. Liberty went for two on the conversion, hoping to pull within a field goal, but their fullback was stopped short.

Shilshole 14, Liberty 9.

The Liberty crowd went crazy and the players were pumped up, smelling the upset victory over the undefeated, ranked team. And they had the momentum back, no doubt about it. Still, there were only five minutes left in the game. If we could run out the clock, we'd have it—a win against a good team on the road.

Carlson put the game on my shoulders. I was still strong, still feeling jacked up, while everyone else was slowing. On first down, I took the ball for eight yards right up the middle, and then went off tackle for seven and a first down on the next play. Four minutes and change left in the game.

The next play was a quick pitch. I'd been cutting back all game long. This time, I went for the corner, never even looking for a lane. I got it, too, and I was in the open field with nothing but green grass ahead of me. Fifty ... forty ... thirty ... twenty ... fifteen ... ten—

That's when I eased up. And that's when their safety—the guy I'd beaten twice—reached in from behind and poked the ball free. It skittered into the end zone, and before I realized what was happening, he flopped on it. In seconds I'd gone from hero to goat; I'd fumbled away the ball—and perhaps the game and the season along with it.

The Liberty safety stood up, the football tucked under his arm, and smirked at me. A black rage came over me, the same black rage I'd felt when DeShawn had brought the penalty flag fluttering in. But the Liberty safety wasn't ninety yards away. The Liberty guy wasn't ten seconds away. There was no time for me to think, to gather control, to pull back. He was right there.

The rage took over.

I knew the play was dead, that it was a touchback, that he couldn't run the ball out of the end zone. I knew those things, but I leveled him anyway—stuck my helmet into his ribs and drove him into the turf, wiping that smirk off his face. He lay on the ground, rolling this way and that, writhing in pain.

Yellow penalty flags flew all around me. Personal foul—fifteen yards: I knew that was coming. But then the ref pointed at me and pointed to the tunnel. I'd been ejected.

"I thought he could run!" I screamed. "I thought he could run!"

The ref turned and walked away. I started after him, but DeShawn intercepted me. A second later Carlson had me by the elbow. "Go to the locker room, Mick," he said. "Now."

A chorus of boos cascaded down from the stands. I

looked back to the field. The trainer from Liberty was out on the field; the player I'd hit was still down, still rolling in pain. In that instant, I knew that what I'd done was out of line—crazy and dangerous—and I was ashamed.

As I walked down the tunnel leading to the locker room, the Liberty fans were up screaming at me, calling me a cheap shot artist and a thug. Somebody threw a Coke in my face.

Once in the locker room, I went straight to a sink, turned on the cold water, and splashed it on my face. What had happened to me? The rage had come so fast and with such fury that I'd been powerless. It had come like a meteor falling from the sky. No, not like a meteor, like a bomb.

I'd been in the locker room about five minutes when Mr. Stimes came in. I was sure he was going to tell me that Liberty had marched down the field and scored, sure that we'd lost because of my idiotic penalty, but Stimes gave me the thumbs-up. "We won," he said.

"That's good," I answered. "Is the guy I hit okay?"

Stimes shrugged. "I'm sure he's felt better, but he walked off on his own power." He paused. "Coach doesn't want you in the locker room when the team gets here. So grab your stuff and get onto the bus."

I sat alone on the bus for half an hour before the team boarded. I took a window seat up front and stared into the street as the guys filed past me. The bus ride back took forty minutes, but it seemed like forty hours. I was certain Carlson would come chew me out—I *wanted* him to come chew me out—but he never even looked at me.

When the bus pulled into the school parking lot, I grabbed my duffel and was the first player off. My Jeep was parked toward the tennis courts. I had it started and was out of the parking lot before ten guys were off the bus.

My dad had been at the game, right on the fifty, his usual spot. I was sure he'd be sitting at the kitchen table. I thought about driving around for a couple of hours to wait him out. But what would have been the point?

I parked in the driveway next to his truck. When I opened the front door, I saw the light in the kitchen. I went in. His eyes were bright with anger. "What was that all about, Mick?" he said. "Have you lost your mind?"

"Does Mom know?"

He shook his head. "No. I told her you had a good game. Which was true, by the way, until you trashed it."

"Will it be in the newspaper tomorrow?"

"I doubt it. Writers go easy on high school kids. But if you pull something like that in college, it'll be on *SportsCenter*. The whole country will see it."

For a while neither of us spoke. Then he waved his hand, dismissing me. "Go to bed. There's nothing to be said."

10

MONDAY MORNING, I was called out of English class to the library annex. When I got there, Carlson was sitting behind a desk. He motioned for me to sit, folded his hands on the desk, and then leaned forward, fixing me with his eye. "I like you, Mick. I like your intensity and effort. You run the way you've shown you're capable of running and nobody will beat us. I'm talking state title. But there's absolutely no room in the game for cheap shots. Do you understand?"

"Yes, sir. I'm sorry for what I did."

"Yeah, well, I'm glad to hear it. But being sorry isn't enough. Actions have consequences, which is why I'm suspending you from the team. You won't play this week."

"But—"

"No discussion, Mick. Go back to class."

．．．

Every afternoon that week I stood along the sidelines in my street clothes. I clapped and called out "Good play!" whenever anyone did something good. I kept a smile on my face, but inside I was tied in knots. I respected Carlson; I respected everything about him. I didn't want him thinking I was some cheap shot artist. I wanted him to respect me. But I wanted to play, too. I wanted to play and I wanted to win. What I needed was time, time to figure it all out. Only a football season doesn't take a time-out; it goes like a whirlwind.

The hardest part was talking with my mom. My dad had been right—the newspapers hadn't reported anything about the ejection. I would have been so embarrassed, so ashamed, if she'd ever found out what I'd done. But because she didn't know, I had to make up some explanation for missing Friday's game. On Wednesday I decided to tell her that I was going to sit out because my ankle was sore. But once I told that lie, she kept asking me about my injury and I had to lie over and over.

11

CARLSON WOULDN'T let me stand along the sidelines, so I watched Friday's game against Bothell from the top row of Memorial Stadium. From up there, I spotted Kaylee and her friends down just behind the band. I thought about going down and sitting with them, but since I'd skipped Heather's party, I was pretty sure they wouldn't want me.

It was tough watching. You play together with guys week after week and suddenly you're not there with them, and a feeling of emptiness comes to you. We needed to keep winning to make it to the playoffs, but there was nothing I could do to help.

We started the game decently. All through the first half, Dave Kane ran hard. On a couple of plays I was sure that if I'd been out there, I could have broken a long one, and then I'd feel sick inside, but Kane kept moving the ball forward, and he didn't fumble. When we did get in third-and-long situations, Drew was on the money with his passes.

We scored the first three times we had the ball. DeShawn hauled in a pass in the corner of the end zone on a fade pattern for our first touchdown. The second drive stalled, but K. J. Solomon kicked a forty-yard field goal, his longest kick of the year, to push the score to 10–0. Early in the second quarter, Kane bulled over from the four-yard line, carrying two Bothell guys into the end zone with him. The extra point made our lead 17–0.

That's when the momentum turned.

Solomon's kickoff was a short line drive. The Bothell returner took it on the dead run, followed the wedge of blockers up the middle, broke left, and was gone. His seventy-yard runback cut the lead to 17–7, and it brought the Bothell players back from the dead.

If we'd been able to sustain a drive and get a touch-down or a field goal or even a couple of first downs, we'd have regained the momentum, but Bothell's defense stuffed Kane on two runs and then batted down Drew's third-down pass. After a short punt, Bothell took over and drove right down the field, scoring on a flanker reverse. Their kicker missed the extra point, so at the half our lead was 17–13.

The third quarter was one of those quarters in which nothing happens. Bothell would get a couple of first downs, then stall because of a penalty or a dropped pass and have to punt. We'd get a couple of first downs, then stall because of a penalty or a dropped pass and have to punt. All we managed was one field goal to push the lead to 20–13.

By the time the fourth quarter began, I was pacing back and forth by the wall at the top of the stadium. I ached to be down on the field, the ball under my arm the blockers pushing forward.

The quarter started ugly: lots of penalties, lots of dropped passes, lots of blown assignments, lots of nothing. But with five minutes left in the game, Drew found DeShawn over the middle with a perfect strike. He had one safety to beat, and for a split second it looked as though he might break into the clear. But the Bothell guy didn't go for DeShawn's move, and as he made the tackle, he stuck his helmet right on the football. It popped loose, and another Bothell player fell on the fumble. Instead of scoring a game-clinching touchdown, we'd turned the ball over near midfield.

"Hold them!" I shouted, and my voice echoed off the wall so loudly that some adults from down below turned and looked up at me. I didn't care. "Hold them!" I shouted again and again.

The Bothell drive ate up the clock—no big plays at all. It was three yards here and four yards there. Twice Bothell converted on fourth-down plays. Their drive was part skill, part luck, and part determination. With thirty-one seconds left, the quarterback punched the ball into the end zone on a sneak. Our lead had shrunk to 20–19.

They'd blown one conversion already, and their kicker looked shaky, so the extra point was anything but automatic. Everyone was up screaming. The snap was good. The placekicker drove forward with his kicking motion. It wasn't until no ball came off his foot that I realized the fake was on. That's when I spotted the holder. He had the ball and was rolling out to his right. In the end zone was a tight end, wide open, with no Shilshole defender within ten yards. It was right there, the two-point conversion, the win, and the end of our run to glory. All the Bothell guy had to do was toss the football to his buddy, the kind of toss he must have made a million times. But with the pressure on, he short-armed it. The ball wobbled out into the flat; the tight end came back for it, diving. He got his hands on it, and for an instant I thought he'd win the game for them with a miracle catch, but the ball hit off his fingertips and bounced harmlessly away. The guy who'd thrown the pass fell to his knees and pounded the ground as our guys jumped around and hugged one another. We'd gotten the win. It had been close, and it had taken luck, but a W is a W.

Foothill was waiting.

12

WHEN I WOKE UP the next morning, I had it all figured out. On Monday, Carlson would reinstate me. I'd work like a demon all week at practice. By game time, I'd be ready, and so would the whole team. I wouldn't take the XTR. I'd be so pumped with adrenaline, I wouldn't need it.

We wouldn't blow them out; Foothill was way too good to be blown out. They would fight us to the end. But in the fourth quarter, I'd get my shot at redemption. There'd be a fourth-down play, fourth and goal, with the game on the line. Carlson would call my number. Foothill would be expecting me; number 50 would be waiting for me. But I'd make it anyway. Somehow, some way, I'd make that final yard.

And Monday afternoon Carlson called me into the coaches' office, exactly as I thought he would. He even said almost exactly what I thought he'd say. "You're back on the team, Mick. Whether you stay on it is up to you."

I left the office and went into the locker room. The guys nodded to me, nobody overly friendly, but nobody turning away, either. I'd never really given much thought to practice; it was just something I did. But the suspension made me realize how much a part of my life it was. Getting the shoulder pads just right, lacing up my cleats, snapping the chin strap—it felt great to be doing the little things again.

On the field, I was the leader. First one in line for every drill, one hundred percent effort. Carlson praised me a couple of times and the guys around me responded, too, pushing their own effort level up. It was all just as I'd pictured it.

And then I got the shock.

When we broke into groups to walk through the plays, Carlson sent me to Coach Brower, who was handling the second team and the special teams. Dave Kane stayed with Drew and DeShawn and the rest of the first team.

I hadn't seen it coming. I should have—it was obvious. I'd screwed up big-time, and Kane had done okay against Bothell. Not great, but he hadn't fumbled the game away. I'd thrown my spot away with my crazy personal foul; Carlson wasn't going to give it back to me. I'd have to earn it.

Only there was no opportunity. Monday, Carlson spent the whole time with the starters. I was forty yards away, running every play as if I were in the Super Bowl, but he didn't see anything. Tuesday we watched Foothill's game against Woodinville for an hour, and the practice afterward was light, no pads at all. Wednesday we had some contact drills, but they were short, and if I did anything to catch Carlson's eye, he didn't mention it. By Thursday doubt was tearing at me. Everything I'd done had been done with my eye on Foothill. He couldn't keep me on the bench. It just couldn't happen.

About an hour into practice, Carlson had Kane walk through the plays—my plays—and he called me over and made me watch, rubbing my nose in it. When the walk-through ended, Drew slid up next to me. "Don't worry, Mick," he said.

"What?" I said.

"Carlson's going to play you. He's aching for a shot at a state title."

"So why am I back on special teams? Why is Kane getting all the reps?"

"He's testing you, making sure you can keep your cool. So long as you don't do anything stupid, you'll play. You won't start, but you'll play."

Carlson blew his whistle. "Special teams practice next," he called out. "Three-quarters speed. Nobody gets hurt."

"I don't think so," I said to Drew.

"Trust me."

Friday morning my dad came down while I was eating breakfast. "So, what do you think? You going to play tonight?"

"I'm not starting."

"But are you going to play?"

"I don't know for sure."

He frowned. "Mick, if you're going to play, I want to be there. Lion understands that. But if you're going to sit on the bench, then I need to be at work. So which is it?"

I sat silently, thinking about what Drew had said. At last I looked up. "I'm going to play."

13

WHEN I PULLED the Jeep into the driveway after school that afternoon, my dad was sitting on the porch with a football in his hand. "I figured you'd be a little tight," he said, "so I thought we could head over to the park, shake out some of the jitters."

I was tight. "Sounds good," I said. "Just let me put my backpack in the house."

It was gray and windy, a tough night for quarterbacks to throw. As my dad tossed the ball to me, he told me not to think about last year's game. "That one is over," he said. "What happened then has no bearing on tonight."

Around four-thirty we returned to the house. I climbed the stairs to my room, put my duffel on the bed, and unzipped it. At the bottom, wrapped up in the towel, was the kit filled with the vials of XTR and all the other stuff. I was about to take it out when my dad knocked on the door, opened it a foot, and leaned in. "You'd better get moving," he said. "If your coach is mad at you already, you don't want to be late."

I shoved my extra socks into the duffel. "I'm going right now," I said.

He stayed, rooted in the doorway, his eyes on me. No way could I pull the kit out without his asking what it was. I zipped my duffel shut, slipped by him, and headed down the stairs.

• • •

When I arrived at Memorial Stadium, the locker rooms hadn't been opened. Drew and DeShawn and a few other guys were standing around out front. I sat down on the curb, my duffel under my knees. Finally the guy with the key showed up. I carried the duffel inside, careful to treat it the same way the rest of the guys treated theirs. As I put on my gear, my heart was pounding like a drum. It would be too unfair to get caught now, when I wasn't even going to use the stuff.

Before every game the adrenaline flows, but this game was like no other. It was a championship game, two undefeated teams, and it was a revenge game, too. As game time neared, guys started hollering encouragement to one another, shouting how this year was our year, hitting shoulder pad to shoulder pad, helmet to helmet. Carlson gave us the final instructions, which were all about not getting too high or too low but to stay on an even keel, because it was going to be a long, hard game against a worthy opponent. It all sounded good, but everybody was already way over the top, including Carlson. Beads of sweat had formed across his forehead, and his nostrils were flared. "One hundred percent effort!" he shouted. "One hundred percent concentration! Now! Now! Now!"

Screaming and howling filled the locker room. My ears were ringing; I couldn't tell my voice from the voices of my teammates. Somebody grabbed hold of me; I turned around—it was DeShawn. His eyes were like saucers; I'd never seen them like that. "It's our turn!" he shouted. "Our turn!"

Somebody grabbed him and spun him around. Then

somebody else started pounding on the lockers, and then everyone was pounding, and the volume kept rising higher and higher, and I was electric from toe to head. This wasn't the game to hold back. Not now, not against Foothill. Everything the team had worked for all season, all off-season, absolutely everything was riding on this one game. It wasn't my brain that decided; it was my body.

I picked up my duffel and headed toward the bathroom.

I went to the last stall, stepped inside, and locked the metal door behind me. I could hear the shouting outside; I knew that soon Carlson would release us through the tunnel. I cleaned my skin, cleaned the needle, and then filled the syringe with the XTR. I pushed the plunger forward, forcing out all the air, not stopping until a few drops of liquid dribbled out. Then I jabbed the needle into my flesh and pushed down. A little more isopropyl alcohol, a quick massage of the injection site, everything back in the duffel—it was done. I took a couple of deep breaths to compose myself. When I felt completely relaxed, I slid the metal locking bar back, pushed the metal door open, and stepped out.

Drew was standing right there, right in front of me,

blocking my way. I felt myself starting to reel, as if I were on a ship in a storm. "What are you doing?" he said.

I don't know how I heard him. The screaming was still going on out in the locker room, and his voice wasn't much more than a whisper. But I heard him.

I gave a confused laugh. "What are you talking about?"

"What's in your duffel?" he said.

"My duffel?"

"Yeah, Mick. Your duffel. What you got in there?"

"What do you think? My street clothes, some tape, a water bottle."

"Yeah? So why bring it to the john?" He motioned with his head toward the stall. "What were you doing in there, Mick?"

My ears were burning, my heart was pounding, but somehow I kept my voice calm. "I was in the john, Drew. What do you think I was doing?"

"Unzip the bag, Mick. Let me see what's inside."

I stared at him, unsure what to do. And then I was saved. Coach Brower leaned his head in the doorway. "Move it, guys. Your teammates are halfway through the tunnel."

Drew turned and headed out to the locker area. I

followed him, found an open locker, shoved my duffel inside, and then ran to the tunnel. A second later I was screaming along with fifty other guys as we raced onto the field.

14

AS WE CAME POURING OUT, our fans rose, cheering as one. A minute later, the Foothill players charged onto the field, and their fans were up and cheering. It was a cold, drizzly night, but the place was alive.

We won the coin toss, so Foothill kicked off. Kane's runback took the ball out past the thirty, and our offense charged onto the field. I reached for my helmet and had nearly pulled it over my head before I remembered: I wasn't starting.

Everything happens fast on a football field, but a running back has to have patience. He has to wait for an opening and then make his move. And he has to be twice as patient in the rain, with the wet turf slowing the linemen, making every play take one beat longer. But Kane couldn't wait, not in a game with this much pressure. He'd take Drew's handoff and just plunge into the line, sometimes running smack into his own blockers. Time and again, possession after possession—the same thing. I was going crazy on the sidelines. Carlson had to see what I was seeing; he had to know what I knew. So when would he yank Kane and put me in?

Near the end of the first quarter Foothill caught lightning in a bottle. On third and inches inside their own twenty, the Spartan quarterback faked a handoff to the fullback. Both of our safeties bit, so when the QB rolled to his right and looked downfield, his wide receiver was open by ten yards. The pass was long and high, giving the receiver plenty of time to run under it. He took it in stride at the forty, and five seconds later he was in the end zone.

Foothill 7, Shilshole 0.

I was sure that touchdown would be my ticket into the game, but Carlson stuck with Kane for another series. We managed a couple of decent plays—both of them passes from Drew to DeShawn. But on third and one from Foothill's forty, Kane smacked into the back of our center and fumbled the wet ball. A Foothill linebacker covered it, and minutes later their kicker split the uprights with a thirty-yard field goal, pushing their lead to 10–0. "Johnson," Carlson called as the ball sailed through, "put your helmet on. You're going in."

He didn't have to say it twice. And once I was on the

field, Carlson didn't mess around: on nearly every play my number was called. Six yards . . . four yards . . . five yards . . . five yards. Foothill's defense was the best in the league, maybe the best in the state, but I was rested and ready and strong, and I had the XTR racing through my bloodstream.

On second and six from their thirty-three, Drew faked a handoff to me. The linebackers were so focused on me that they had all come up, leaving our tight end wide open over the middle. Drew's pass was on the money, and Jones rumbled all the way until he hit pay dirt. Our fans went crazy as the band struck up the fight song. We blew the extra point, so at halftime the score was Foothill 10, Shilshole 6.

The Foothill guys got their legs back at the half, and they were stronger off the line in the third quarter. I ran hard, but our blocking wasn't consistent. If I had a sliver of a hole, I'd break a five- or seven-yard run. But if there's nothing there, there's nothing there. Our drives stalled and we had to punt.

Sometime in the third quarter, the drizzle had become a steady, chilling rain. My body was somehow frozen from the rain at the same time it was hot from my sweat. I didn't let myself feel my own misery. I kept pounding the ball at them, pounding it and pounding it. Early in the fourth quarter, the left side of their defensive line broke. I sliced through them for eight yards, then twelve, then six. I thought Carlson would run right, or maybe throw a pass, but he came back with another running play left. I broke into the secondary and then cut back. A cornerback went for an ankle tackle that I stepped out of. A safety missed me and I was gone, down the sideline and into the end zone for the touchdown that put us ahead. This time Solomon made the extra point, so with seven minutes left in the game, the score was Shilshole 13, Foothill 10.

We were just about there, just about in the state playoffs.

Our fans, dry under the overhang, were on their feet, cheering our defense. The Foothill coach could feel the game slipping away, and a little desperation crept into his play calling. There was time for him to stick to his game plan and run a balanced attack, but on the next series, all the plays were passes. Foothill clicked on the first one, a bullet over the middle for fifteen yards. But the next two were little dink jobs in the flat that gained six yards total, setting up third and four.

Carlson guessed pass and sent the two outside linebackers on a blitz. He was right—but it wasn't the blitz that blew up the play. The Spartan quarterback lost his footing in the mud before any of our guys reached him. He lost eight yards, making it fourth and twelve. The punting team came onto the field and kicked the ball away.

We took over on our own thirty-three-yard line with less than five minutes left. All we needed were a couple of first downs, and the way to get them was to have me run the ball right down their throats. Carlson knew it and called my number three straight times. I got us a first down; more important, the game clock kept ticking: 3:28 . . . 3:27. . . 3:26 . . .

All Carlson had to do was keep calling plays for me. It didn't matter that Foothill was stacking the line. I could still gain yards. I had the strength; I knew I had it.

Instead, when he saw eight Foothill guys crowding the line of scrimmage, he decided to go for the knockout. The call was for a bomb to DeShawn on a fly pattern. Drew took the snap, faked a handoff to me, and dropped back to pass. The play might have worked, but as Drew released the ball he was blind-sided by a defensive end. The ball fluttered into the night air like a wounded duck. The cornerback covering DeShawn cut underneath him and made the interception on a dead run, and then he was off—down the sideline.

Touchdown.

Drew was down from the hit, and he stayed lying in that cold muck for a couple of minutes. When he finally got up, he was holding his right shoulder and grimacing as Stimes led him to the locker room.

Foothill's band was playing their fight song over and over; their fans were delirious; their entire team had poured into the end zone to swarm the cornerback who'd scored the touchdown. Their coaches were trying to get them out of the end zone, but it was too late. Yellow penalty flags for excessive celebration were all over the field. The extra point made the score 17–13, but instead of kicking off from the forty, the penalty pushed them back to their twenty-five.

That's when Kane came through. He fielded the kick on our thirty-five. Instead of messing around with fancy moves this way and that, he brought the ball straight upfield. We had a great wedge and he made it all the way to Foothill's forty before he was brought down.

There was 2:52 left.

Plenty of time.

With Drew in the locker room, our quarterback was Tom McGinley, a tall, skinny senior. When I first saw him at tryouts, I'd thought he was the water boy. It turned out he was a good athlete; he just didn't have size. He could do everything on a football field but survive the hits.

Carlson didn't panic and have McGinley try to do more than he could. Instead, he stayed with me. The ball was slick, so I had to be extra careful to tuck it away and to hold it tight. This was not the time for a fumble. A sweep left for eight yards . . . 2:40 . . . 2:39. A little screen pass, not much more than a handoff, for seven more. A draw play for six that got us into the red zone . . . 1:51 . . . 1:50 . . . 1:49.

Everybody in the stadium knew I was getting the ball on every play. Foothill's coach assigned a linebacker to bird-dog me. It didn't matter. On a quick draw I drove down inside the ten for a first and goal with just over a minute left.

But then, on first down and goal, McGinley fumbled the snap. For a second I thought a Foothill guy would recover, but when it squirted free from him, our left guard fell on it back in the slop on the twelve-yard line. We had to use our second time-out to regroup.

When we huddled, McGinley's eyes were scared. "Just watch the snap into your hands and then stick the ball out for me," I said.

On the next play, I went off tackle to the six, and on third down swept wide right, taking the ball down to the three-yard line.

Fourth down.

We took our final time-out. I sucked down some water as we huddled around Carlson. "Thirty-four toss sweep on one," he said. "Linemen, hold your blocks." Then Carlson looked at McGinley. "Make a nice smooth toss and Mick will take it to the house."

The referee blew his whistle. We huddled up, and McGinley repeated what Carlson had called. "Thirty-four toss sweep on one." Guys clapped and trotted to the line of scrimmage. I liked that the snap was on *one*, liked that there was no waiting around, liked that it was *now*.

"Hut!" McGinley called, and the center snapped the ball.

The pitchout was right on the money. I watched the ball into my hands, tucked it away against my chest, and then drifted down the line, looking for a crack. And there it was, a small opening between the guard and the tackle. I cut upfield, but right then a Foothill linebacker shed his blocker. It was number 50, the same guy who'd brought me down the year before. He hit me at the one-yard line. For a split second we were both frozen, both straining, neither yielding. But this time it was his legs that gave way, this time I drove him back, and a second later I was churning forward, across the goal line and into the end zone. I raised both arms high above my head, reaching the football toward the sky, the rain pouring down on me like diamonds.

15

WE'D JUST WON THE TITLE, but in the locker room afterward, there wasn't much hollering and cheering, because we were all too dog-tired to scream. I looked around for Drew and I found him by Mr. Stimes. I thought he'd be hurting, but he looked okay. "How you feeling?" I said.

He nodded. "I'm fine. A stinger is all it was. I couldn't feel my arm for a few minutes there, and then the feeling came back."

"So you'll be able to play next week?"

"I could play right now." He paused. "Mick—"

Just then Carlson stood up on a chair and blew his whistle. "Listen up, gentlemen. We've got the back room at Chicago's rented," he shouted. "The booster club is paying, so get into your street clothes and get over there before the pizza gets cold. Five-minute walk."

DeShawn came up. "You heard the man," he said to Drew. "Let's get a move on."

Drew turned to me. "We'll talk later."

"Sure," I said, and I moved back to my locker area.

Guys dressed quickly and headed for the door in groups of three and four. I stood, looking around; nobody had asked me to join them. McGinley noticed. "Come with us, Mick," he said, and he motioned for me to join up with him and his friends.

As I was walking up Mercer Street, I felt a hand squeeze my shoulder. I turned, and there was my dad. "Great game," he said, his smile wide.

. . .

At the pizza place, I sat with McGinley and a couple of other second-stringers. They'd hardly played, but they were still flying—talking loud and eating fast. I tried to get caught up in their excitement. Maybe I could have, if it hadn't been for Drew. He was with DeShawn and Middleton and Jones, but he might as well have been by himself. Every time I glanced over, he was looking straight ahead, his face expressionless.

A little before midnight, DeShawn banged his knife against his glass. "Let's hear it for our touchdown machine! Let's hear it for Mick!" The guys started hollering.

Then Middleton jumped on a chair. "Let's hear it for our coach!" he screamed, and the hollering went up another notch. After that, a bunch of different guys called out other people's names until finally one of the assistant coaches shouted: "Let's hear it for everybody!"

The pizza guys stopped bringing out new pizzas and started cleaning up. "Party's over," Carlson said.

I stood up, shook a few people's hands, and then headed back to the school parking lot where I'd left the Jeep. I thought about offering a ride to Drew or McGinley or somebody, but I wanted to be alone. They'd all managed to get there without me; they'd find a way home.

Fifteen minutes later I pulled into the driveway. The house was dark. I opened the front door and quietly walked upstairs, careful not to wake up my mom or dad. Up in my room, I opened the duffel. I wanted to get the syringe and the XTR back into the safety of my closet. I fumbled around, feeling for the stuff, but I couldn't find it. I flicked the light on and dumped everything out.

No vial. No syringe. No needle.

That's when my cell phone rang.

16

IT WAS DREW, just as I knew it would be. "We've got to talk," he said.

"I'll pick you up in five minutes," I said. "Be in front of your house."

I closed the phone. My head started spinning, the ground seemed to open underneath my feet, and all of a sudden I could feel myself starting to fall.

I closed my eyes to calm myself. Then I pulled my shoes on and put on a black jacket. I'd started down the stairs when I stopped. I turned around, went back up-stairs into the computer room and over to the book-case. Bottom shelf. Far left. I fumbled around for a minute or two, and then I had it.

It was after one in the morning. There was a car here and there on the road, but most of the world seemed asleep. When I turned onto Drew's street, I spotted him under a streetlight in front of his house. I pulled up and opened the door for him. "Your parents know you're meeting me?" I asked as he slipped in next to me. My voice sounded wrong to me, like someone else's voice.

"Be real, Mick."

I drove down to Golden Gardens Park. The police always lock the main gate at eleven-thirty, so I pulled into the overflow parking lot. You can get to the beach through the tunnel from there. "Let's go down by the ponds," I said.

We walked in the silent darkness past the green fields that led to the two ponds just above the beach. It wasn't until we'd reached them and were leaning on the railing and looking out over one of the ponds that he spoke. "You're using steroids, right? The syringe and all that."

"Yeah, I'm using steroids."

He shook his head. "Why? That stuff causes cancer and liver damage and all sorts of other weird crap, and you know it."

"I use steroids because I have to," I said, saying out loud what I'd never before been able to admit, not even to myself. "I use them because without them I'm not good enough."

He shook his head and snorted in disgust. "You're plenty good enough. But now this whole season, everything we supposedly did, it's all ruined. You cheated, Mick. You were the main man, and you flat-out cheated. We don't belong in the playoffs; we didn't win a thing."

We stared out at the water for a long time. "What are you planning to do?" I said at last.

"The only thing I can do. I'm going to Carlson."

"Don't do it, Drew."

He turned toward me. The anger vanished from his voice. "Mick, you need help. Carlson's been around. He's a good guy. He'll know the right thing to do. About you, about the season, about everything."

I had no chances left. Everything was going to end. This year, next year. Forever. I was falling fast and I had to grab hold of something, anything, to stop the fall. I put my hand in my pocket and felt the metallic coldness of the gun. "You can't go to Carlson," I said, my voice as icy as the revolver. "You can't tell him. You can't tell anybody."

"Mick, I've got to be able to look myself in the mirror. I'm letting you know now because I don't want you to think I went behind your back. You can talk forever, but nothing is going to change my mind."

He started back along the path to the parking lot. My head was pounding as if my skull weren't large enough to hold my brain. I took a couple of quick steps toward him and then called his name. "Drew. Stop."

He turned back.

I pulled out the revolver and pointed it at him.

He peered through the darkness at me. "What is that, Mick?" he said. "Is that a gun? Are you going to shoot me?"

I let my hand drop to my side. "Just promise me you'll keep your mouth shut and nothing will happen."

"Are you going to shoot me and throw my body into this little duck pond? Is that your solution?"

"Promise me, Drew."

"Look at yourself. Look what the stuff has done to you."

"Promise me."

He turned and started walking again. I raised the gun and pointed it at him. "Stop!" I yelled.

But he didn't stop. I aimed, and then aimed again, but I couldn't pull the trigger.

Then, in a flash, I knew why I gone back upstairs for the gun. It had never been to shoot Drew. A strange sort of peace came over me, the same peace I'd felt when I'd thought about swimming out into the black water. The anger went away. The fear went away. I put the revolver to my temple, felt the coldness of the muzzle there, took a deep breath, took another one, and pulled the trigger.

EPILOGUE

1

You wouldn't think it would take much skill to shoot yourself in the head, but I didn't even do that right. I must have jerked the barrel upward just as I'd done those first few times at the gun range. Instead of crashing into my brain, all the bullet did was tear off part of my scalp and burn lots of my hair. I bled all over the place, but I didn't die.

Drew carried me to the Jeep and drove me to Ballard Hospital, or so they tell me. I remember coming to the next morning and finding myself in a strange room, my head wrapped in bandages, an IV in my arm, my mom asleep in a chair by my bed, my dad sitting on the floor, his forehead resting on his knees. As I was looking down at him, he raised his head and our eyes caught. "Hey, Mick," he said.

That woke my mother and she turned toward me. Her eyes were red-rimmed and her face looked old.

"Hi, Mom," I whispered.

She stood and leaned forward, put her face next to mine, and kissed me on the cheek.

I looked again to my father. He looked down at the floor, then stood and came over to the other side of the bed. He took my hand, his grip tight. "You feeling all right?" he asked.

"I'm okay."

"You should have come to us, Mick. To me or to your mom. You're not alone in this world. You've never been alone, and you never will be—not as long as either of us is alive."

My chest tightened. I was on the verge of sobbing, but I fought back the tears. *There's no crying in football.* That's what he'd said to me in the backyard all those years ago, and—crazy as it seems—those were the words that came to me then.

"I'm sorry," I managed.

My mom reached down and squeezed my hand. She forced herself to smile. "Everything's going to be okay. I know it's hard for you to believe, but it's true. Maybe not today or tomorrow, but you'll get through this. We'll be here to help, every step of the way."

She looked at me then, her eyes expectant. She was waiting for me to say something, but no words seemed right. Just then a nurse looked in. "Is he awake?" she asked, and without waiting for an answer she disappeared down a hallway.

A few minutes later a doctor came in, asked me questions, and shined a light in each eye. "He may lose a little hearing in his right ear," he told my parents, "but even that's not definite." Then he looked to me. "You're a very lucky young man."

After he left, my mom and dad sat, each on one side of me. We talked about the room and we talked about the hospital and we talked about the doctor. We talked about everything except what I had done and what was going to happen next.

A woman brought me breakfast and a nurse took my temperature and adjusted the IV. After that, my mom and dad went down to the cafeteria. "We'll give you some time to rest," my mom said as they left.

When they were with me, I'd thought that I wanted to be alone. Once they were gone, I wanted them back. I lowered the bed and closed my eyes, but that was no good. So then I raised the bed and looked out into the corridor, watching the nurses walk this way and that, seeing patients wheeled in and out.

After an hour or so, my mom and dad returned. They told me about their breakfast and a vending machine that was jammed. "A policeman will be coming later," my dad said after a long silence. "He'll be asking you questions about last night. When he comes, your mom and I are going to leave. Tell him everything, Mick. Don't hold back."

Once he said that, they talked about a vacation in San Diego over Christmas. "A little sun and warm weather would be good for us," my mother said. Then they discussed other places we might go instead— Arizona or Florida or even Hawaii. As they talked, I kept looking into the corridor, awaiting the policeman. But when he finally showed, I barely noticed him. I'd imagined someone big, in uniform, gun dangling at his hip. Instead, the policeman was a slender Asian man, about fifty. "I'm Lee Ikeda," he said. "Seattle Police."

He shook my dad's hand, then my mom's, and then nodded toward me. They talked some about the hospital, and as they spoke I felt my throat tightening and a dizziness coming over me. "I'd like to speak to Mick alone," he said at last. My mom came to the bed and kissed me again; my dad gave me a smile.

Once they were gone, Mr. Ikeda took out a notepad and a pen. "I've just come from Popeye's," he said. "We've got Peter Volz nailed solid. So why don't you just tell me how all this happened?"

I looked at him; I looked at the IV in my arm. I put

my hand to my head and felt the bandages. I thought of my mom and my dad, of Drew and Coach Carlson, of Aaron Clark and Matt Drager. Everything that I'd been holding down came surging up, a tidal wave I couldn't stop.

"I don't know how it happened," I whispered. "I don't know." Then I covered my face with my hands to hide my tears.

2

I SPENT THAT NIGHT at the hospital, and the next morning my parents brought me here, to the drug rehabilitation center. I didn't want to come, but I didn't have much choice. If I complete the rehab program, my file gets sealed. Unless I screw up again, it will almost be as if none of this ever happened. If I want, I can even play football again next year. But if I don't complete this program, then I go into the court system and everything is out in the open. I don't want that, and neither do my mom and my dad or Mr. Ikeda.

On the way here, we drove past the old Norwegian cemetery. When I was in middle school, we used to dare one another to walk through the cemetery. My dad looked over at me as we passed those graves, and I knew what he was thinking, because I was thinking the same thing. A twitch was all that had kept me alive.

He pulled into the driveway and we got out—all three of us—and looked at the center where I'd be living for three weeks. This place looks like a Spanish mission. All the buildings have red tile roofs and cream stucco walls that would fit in Mexico or Texas but don't really fit in Seattle. Maybe that's the point. Maybe they want me to feel as though I'm a long way from home.

We walked up the pathway, climbed the tile stairs, and pushed open the heavy oak door. At the reception desk across the lobby was an older woman. She asked my name, gave my mom and dad forms on clipboards, and then pointed to a couple of red chairs and a sofa over by a big window. As they filled out the paperwork, I stared at an oak door with a sign reading PATIENTS AND STAFF ONLY on it. I pictured the guys living in the rooms behind that door. They'd be meth addicts and heroin addicts and cocaine addicts.

After ten minutes or so, a tall, fair-haired man wearing glasses came out from behind that door. He strode across the tile floor, walked directly up to me, and stuck out his hand. "Hello, Mick," he said. "I'm Mr. Jonas Riley. I will be your primary counselor while you're here." Next he turned to my mom and dad. They introduced themselves, and the three of them talked about the program and what my days would be like. Then came a moment when everyone stopped talking. It lasted for a while before Mr. Riley said, "I think it's time I showed Mick his room."

"I'm not a drug addict or anything like that," I said, panic coming over me. "I want you to know that up front. It was steroids—that's all I ever used. I don't drink or do marijuana or even smoke cigarettes. Just steroids. So I won't really need drug counseling."

Mr. Riley nodded. "Mick, all I want to do right now is get you settled. You're going to be here awhile; we'll have time to figure out what you do and don't need."

My dad gave me a hug and then stepped back. I turned to my mom. She was teary-eyed. "It'll be okay," I said. She wrapped her arms around me, hugging me tight as if I were a little boy, and I hugged her back the same way. It was the first time I'd hugged her like that in a long, long time.

Mr. Riley started across the tile floor and I followed. We'd taken a few steps when my mother's voice rang out. "Wait, Mick," she said. "There's something I want you to have." She looked to Mr. Riley. "It's in the car. It'll just take a minute. Please."

"There is no hurry, Mrs. Johnson," Mr. Riley said. "We can wait."

When she came back she was holding the large leather-bound Bible that always sits on the table by the sofa. "Sometimes when I'm feeling lost," she said as she handed it to me, "I'll open the book and read and before long I'll find a passage that will comfort me."

I think she was expecting me to tell her I didn't want her Bible, and any other day of my life I probably would have, but that day I took it.

3

IT'S OKAY HERE during the daytime. I get up at eight, eat breakfast, and shoot some hoops by myself out on the asphalt. After that I have my first counseling session with Riley. Pretty soon it's time for lunch, and then some classes, which are easy, because most of the guys in here can barely read. Next comes my second session with Riley, followed by more basketball, and then dinner. I'm ten days into the program, which means I have ten days to go. I get the feeling I'm sort of a star patient; Riley always says that he looks forward to our sessions.

I think I know why he likes me. Most of the guys in here kid themselves. I hear them blaming their parents, blaming the world. I started out doing the same thing. I spent my first four days with Riley putting it all on my dad, saying that if he hadn't pushed me so hard, I would never have done what I did, which I guess is partly true. But only partly. Because Peter was right, way back in the beginning. I'd done it for me.

I wanted to be a star.

Me.

For myself.

Peter had made me say it out loud then, and I'm not running from it now. I put myself in here, and I know what I've got to do when I get out. I've got to live the truth. That's what Riley has been drilling into me, session after session. Lies don't protect you; they just make things worse. He says that lying is like a spear with points on both sides, and that the wounds go deep on both sides.

Today Riley asked me how I'd feel if it turned out that I wasn't good enough to be a star running back. "This Dave Kane, what if he's simply better than you?"

"Then I'll be second string," I said.

"Do you think you can live with that?" he asked.

"I won't like it," I said, "but if that's what I have to do, then that's what I have to do."

In the daytime, it all seems pretty clear.

But then comes the night.

After dinner, most of the guys hang out in the rec room shooting pool. I tried joining them, but I don't fit. So when I finish eating, I come back to this room, take a shower, and brush my teeth. I do everything I can to kill time, but it's never later than nine when I run out of things to do, and there's no way I can go to sleep at nine. At home I'd watch TV or play a video game and the time would pass. But there's nothing in my room here, nothing but the Bible my mom gave me the day I came in.

When I unpacked my stuff that first day, I put the Bible in the bottom drawer of the dresser. I probably would have forgotten about it if it weren't for the kid down the hall. Around eleven on my first night here, he started screaming and crying. The doors and walls between him and me muffled the sound, which somehow made the crying seem as if it were coming from deep inside me. That's when I pulled out the Bible.

It's a big Bible with gold-edged pages and a dark blue leather cover. As soon as I started flipping through the pages, I remembered back to when I was little and my mom used to sit with me on the sofa and read me stories. "You'll like this one," she'd say, and then she'd read about Adam and Eve, or Cain and Abel, or Jacob and Esau.

Four nights ago I read the story of Judas Iscariot and how he betrayed Jesus for thirty pieces of silver. As soon as I started reading about Judas, I thought of Drew. I didn't want to think of him, but I couldn't stop myself. Ever since that night, I've been trying to read something new, or not read at all, but once that kid starts crying, I pull out the Bible, and once I pull out the Bible, I always turn to the story of Judas.

Riley says Drew saved me, and so do my mom and my dad. They say I owe my life to him. And in the daytime, I know they're right. I know how much I owe him. He acted the way a friend is supposed to act. In the daytime I know all that.

But sitting here in the dark with that kid down the hall crying and crying—I'm not sure that Drew saved me. Sometimes I even think that he betrayed me, just as Judas betrayed Jesus. A few more weeks, and I'd have led us to the championship. And if we won the title this year, why not next year? And the year after that? We could have been three-time state champions; both Drew and I could have been all-state players; Coach Carlson could have won the title he was aching to win.

All those good things, if Drew had stayed out of it.

What I told Riley about being second string? When I said it, I meant it. And I want it to be true. But I don't know if it is true. I don't know if I can stand watching Dave Kane play running back while I sit on the bench. I don't know if I can stand feeling myself become smaller, slower, and weaker.

I don't know if I can stand being ordinary.

Every session Riley asks me what I want my life to look like when I get out of here. There's nothing special about my answers. I tell him I want to hang out with Drew and DeShawn in the lunchroom, making jokes and talking loud. I want to play flag football at Crown Hill Park in the rain, sliding through the mud on every tackle. I want to walk around Green Lake with Kaylee, sometimes talking, sometimes quiet, the sun bright in the sky. And I tell him that come next September, I want to be in the locker room before a football game—not sneaking off to a bathroom stall, not hiding anything—just there, with my teammates— just one of the guys.

And that is what I do want. It really is.

But what you want and what you get aren't always the same.

. . .

Before all this happened, I'd read in the newspaper about pro athletes who got caught using steroids. Some of them would pile up two or three or even four substance abuse violations. They'd lose millions of dollars, their reputations, even their careers. It made no sense to me then. They just seemed stupid beyond belief.

They don't seem so stupid now.

Because what I don't tell Riley is that something else is pulling me, drawing me like a magnet draws iron filings. I know that once I'm out of here, I could get in my Jeep and drive to Popeye's, or to the gym up in Shoreline, or to half a dozen other gyms in the city. I could do it any time of the day, any day of the year. Within an hour I could hook up with someone who could get me going on the juice again. Sixty minutes, and I could be back on steroids, getting bigger, faster, and stronger every day. Thinking about it makes my heart race.

So here I am, right this minute, sitting in the dark at midnight on a strange bed in a strange room in a strange place. I know the person I want to become, but I don't know if I can pull it off. I think I can; sometimes I even pray that I can. But the kid down the hall has started screaming again, and in my head I'm screaming, too.

THE END

Check out these other hard-hitting paperbacks:

The Astonishing Adventures of Fanboy and Goth Girl
by Barry Lyga

Boy Toy
by Barry Lyga

Dunk
by David Lubar

Beautiful City of the Dead
by Leander Watts

Runner
by Carl Deuker

Real Time
by Pnina Moed Kass

3 NBs of Julian Drew
by James M. Deem

New Boy
by Julian Houston